I0771172

Red Fern Press

Double Digits. Copyright © 2025 by Steph West. All rights reserved. Printed in the United States of America. No part of this book may be used or reproduced in any manner without written permission except in the case of brief quotations embodied in critical articles and reviews. For permissions, address correspondence to Red Fern Press, 3136 Kingsdale Center, #103, Columbus, OH 43221.

Red Fern Press books may be purchased for educational, business, or sales promotional use. For more information, please e-mail the marketing department at redfernpressquery@gmail.com.

First Edition

ISBN 978-1-967038-01-5 (Kindle)
ISBN 978-1-967038-02-2 (Paperback)

To all my readers.
You're perfect as you are.

Content

Suggestions for Further Reading

On Fire by Steph West (Red Fern Press, 2023)

Newcross by Steph West (Red Fern Press, 2024)

Coming Soon

Book 2 of the *Double Digits* series, *California Love*, by Steph West

Book 2 of the *Newcross* trilogy, *Bounty*, by Steph West

Double Digits

Double Digits Pocket Romance Series

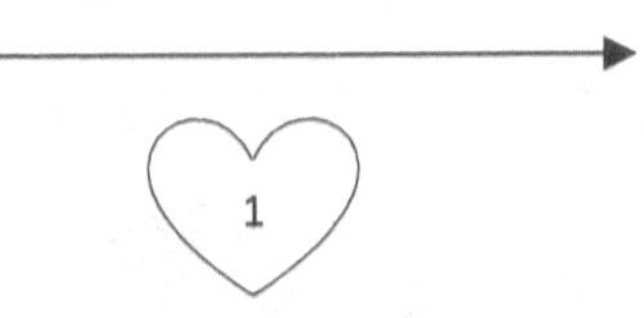

1

A Perfect Fit

Scout held her head high and carried her five-foot, eight-inch frame straight, shoulders back, as she sailed through the hallways of Double Digits headquarters in downtown Pittsburgh. Her power heels clicked the shiny black floors of the twenty-story building with authority as she sashayed her ample curves past the C-suite hallway. She glanced toward Pappy's office. Scout knew the CEO better than anyone, except maybe his own grandsons.

"Hey," Scout said as she caught the eye of Pappy's assistant, Amber. Amber was a stoic, smart, twenty-five-year-old, and not much younger than Scout was. That younger viewpoint was something the company desperately needed right now.

"Good morning," Amber said warmly as Scout walked by. Scout was twenty-eight and had sped through the ranks of the fashion world at a remarkable pace. Her passion for the business combined with her work ethic were a huge part of that upswing.

Pappy had taken notice five months ago and hired her as a consultant on the spot. Now it was June and Scout had quickly become Pappy's right-hand woman. *And sometimes like his granddaughter.* She grinned at the notion as she delicately wiped sweat from her brow and put her Chanel bag on the large desk in her corner office. *Hot today.*

The sunlight streamed through her large windows. She loved the sweeping view of the three rivers where the Monongahela River met the Allegheny and formed the Ohio River. She could see down into Point

State Park at its juncture and enjoyed watching all the people.

She smoothed down her black, sleek Calvin Klein dress and readjusted the straps on her Manolo Blahniks as she got a peek at the photograph on her wall. Australia, one of her favorite places to visit. *Hot as hell. But beautiful.*

That was the main perk of this consultant gig. She could come and go as she pleased, travel on a whim to her favorite places, and then do the hard work of helping Paps move his company into the future of plus-sized clothing for women as he needed her.

Paps, with his thick, gray, sculpted mane and fit frame, was desperate to reach a younger, contemporary audience before he transitioned the company to one of his grandsons, Josh or Lucas. The old man was a spitfire who loved those boys more than they probably realized. *Paps is such a gem.*

She straightened up, brushed her long, chocolate brown hair off her shoulders, and pondered her future once Pappy decided which one of the men took over.

Joshua, thirty-one, was the oldest, and seemed like the best choice, according to Paps. Josh had an MBA and had worked his way up through the company. He was a *responsible* man, as Paps would say. She got the same impression from the tall, dark-haired, clean-shaven heir with a great smile. She'd found him attractive, like everyone, but hadn't interacted with him at Pappy's request.

"I want to understand it myself before we bring them in," he'd said. "Especially Josh."

And then he'd given her a smile as if keeping her hidden in plain sight had something to do with her *and* Joshua. But she'd never asked Paps to clarify that mischievous twinkle in his gray-blue eyes.

Unfortunately, according to Paps, Joshua had a soft heart that came at the expense of Double Digits' bottom line. For the four months Josh managed it, and before Lucas came on board, they'd gone in the red. Add to that the fact that Josh was a bit of a "skinny girls only" skirt-chaser like his father and, according to Paps, he didn't know "a damn thing about plus-sized women."

There was one exception, Paps had said, "Josh loved his grandma more than life itself." Bessie, Pappy's wife, was the woman the company was built for. And now, after losing her valiant fight with breast cancer, it was her legacy.

"That's what makes Josh a contender," Paps had told her. "His genuine love and respect for my Bessie, and what this company meant to her."

Scout picked up this quarter's *Digits* magazine from her glass-top desk and admired her handiwork. *Digits* was a branded magazine emailed to the top ten percent of customers every three months. It was also distributed inside their stores. It was one of the projects Scout had consulted on with Paps. She had done a good job at mixing creative, sales, marketing, and business opportunities into a compelling visual and editorial issue.

God, I love this work.

She grinned like someone just handed her a gold medal as she traced the gorgeous cover with its stunning full-figured, auburn model. *Total win.*

She put the magazine down and headed for her own assistant, Belle. Scout shivered at the blast of A.C., then rubbed her arms for warmth as she contemplated grandson number two: Lucas.

Also cute. But much wilder.

Lucas was fresh out of the University of Pittsburgh's law school, slightly shorter than Josh, and younger at age twenty-nine. He was also lighter in spirit and appearance with sandy blonde hair and light eyes. Lucas was always dressed as sharp as a tack and was an equal opportunity skirt-chaser for any shape, size, or color of any woman who caught his fancy, so said the rumor mill.

"Ahh, my Lucas," Paps had said to her with a guffaw. "He's one crazy kid, huh?"

Paps told her Lucas was a man who would do or say anything to close a deal. "He's a shark."

Lucas's approach over the last few months had given Paps the healthiest bottom line Double Digits had ever seen.

Scout was aware of how Lucas's influence had turned the tide. This latest issue already had the highest sales

conversions of clothing and accessories the
company had ever seen from the magazine.
All of it thanks to Lucas's deals with fresh,
new designers and creative advertising
packages and partnerships.

"He's brilliant," Paps had said. Scout
thought so, too. Though she wasn't entirely
sure Lucas wouldn't sell his own family if it
meant closing a deal. A quality she didn't
love. Plus, office gossip claimed the boys
still behaved like competitive teenagers with
each other, mostly started by Lucas and
ending with Josh. Scout wasn't keen on an
immature boss.

Paps claimed Lucas's shortcomings as his
own. "He was always closer to me than
Bessie. To his detriment."

In Scout's opinion, either of the men
could run the company, though admittedly
their strengths were very different. Josh
could learn the numbers game; she wasn't

sure Lucas could learn to be gentle. Ideally, they'd run it together and balance each other out. It would depend, of course, on what Pappy's vision was for his company and where he wanted it to go.

But if it was up to Scout, she'd rather work for Josh. *Or be on a leadership track myself for the C-Suite.*

Scout was certain she had a handle on the direction Pappy envisioned. She'd been working nonstop with him since January and loved every minute of it.

Once Pappy had seen her ideas and implemented them, the company enjoyed huge boosts and returns. So, really, it was her and Lucas, together, that had given the company its healthiest bottom line.

She could tell Pappy understood that fact and was thinking she deserved more at this company.

I agree.

Scout had never considered settling into a company before, except maybe StudioX, the leading plus-sized fashion company in the world, but Double Digits felt different for some reason.

For the first time since she started consulting and traveling, she felt the urge to settle down for a bit. That was likely coming from the work she did here and maybe even from Paps, who had become as much like a grandfather to her as he was to his own grandsons.

"Hi Scout." She glanced over to see who had interrupted her thoughts. It was Pappy's attorney, Alex. He strode toward the founder's office. *Wait, what's Alex doing here?*

"Hi Alex." She gave him a smile, but it was underscored by curiosity. Alex wasn't the company's general counsel; he was Pappy's personal attorney. He rarely made appearances, so when he did, you took notice. "Going to see Paps?"

"Yep," he said briskly. He gave her a warm smile and then disappeared down the hall to Pappy's office without offering up anything else. *Typical attorney.* She made a mental note of his presence before nodding to her own assistant.

"Morning, Belle," she said. She leaned against the lovely woman's small desk just outside her own office.

"Morning, boss," she said sweetly. Belle, unlike Amber, was much older than Scout. Belle was in her sixties, and gorgeous. Her sleek gray and white hair was shaped in waves around her face. It flowed down to her shoulders as her bright blue eyes sparkled.

Belle was a retired nurse who wanted something different and flexible. Scout was impressed with her work, but, really, she loved Belle because Belle treated her more like family than a boss.

"Did you see Alex?" Scout asked.

"I did," Belle said quietly. She leaned forward, her sleek silver blouse crinkling as she moved. "Wonder why."

"Me, too," Scout whispered. "So, what's on the agenda today?"

"Meetings," Belle quipped. She leaned back and smoothed down her fitted black leggings. Her turquoise bangles clinked like fine China as she did. "A post-mortem on this month's *Digits*, which is on fire. Tons of sales."

"That's great," said Scout.

"It is," she responded. Belle twisted her three-karat wedding ring with her long fingers that bore hot-pink-polished nails. It was a habit she had when she started talking about something serious.

"Paps wants to talk about your contract tomorrow morning," she whispered. "It expires in a month. I scheduled you some prep time today."

"I really appreciate that, Belle," Scout said. "Thank you."

"Sure," she said warmly. She suddenly dropped below her desk, then stood up with a small, brightly colored tin in her hands. She handed it to Scout. "Cookies."

She winked as Scout took the small tin and fingered the gold accents against the teal and red abstract design. "Belle, thank you."

Scout felt nothing but love from Belle. Something she desperately needed. Her own parents were caring, of course, and they loved her, she knew that, but they weren't exactly warm. It had made Scout fiercely independent, and able to do a lot without much coddling, but she'd always wished for just a touch more tenderness in her life.

"I'm gonna go grab a coffee. Want me to get you one, too, to have with the cookies?" Belle asked.

"You know what?" Scout said. "Let me get you a coffee today. I'd like to stop by wardrobe and make-up and see how the next magazine shoot is going. You take yours black with one sweetener, right?"

"You got it," she said. "Thanks."

"No problem," Scout answered. She quickly headed toward the elevator. "I'll be back."

"Take your time," Belle answered. She sat down in her comfy desk chair and got to work.

Scout took the opportunity to peer down the hallway at Pappy's office. Alex was still there. She wrinkled her nose.

Just what exactly is Alex doing here? And does it have anything to do with my contract?

<h1 style="text-align:center">2</h1>

<h2 style="text-align:center">The Ladies Like It</h2>

Josh peered at his shaved face in the rearview mirror as he sat in his white Jeep Cherokee and double-checked his appearance. He licked his finger and smoothed his eyebrows to ensure he was perfectly coifed. Approving his own reflection, he stepped out, locking the Jeep behind him.

He couldn't remember when he started taking such careful measures with the way he looked but he knew it had to do with his grandfather. The man was a perfectionist, right down to the silver tie pin he wore every day of his business life since he started Double Digits. *Grams bought him that tie pin.*

Josh smiled to himself as his long strides led him to the private elevator that went straight to the C-Suite. He reached out to push the elevator button but paused as he listened carefully.

The sound of the company helicopter beginning to land on the roof echoed in the private garage. *Lucas.* He quickly pushed the elevator button once, twice, three times.

"Come on," he whispered urgently.

As soon as the elevator doors opened, he sprinted in and pounded the button for the top floor.

Come on, come on.

Josh impatiently checked his Rolex watch as he stared at the elevator numbers slowly clicking to the top.

"Seriously?" he smirked.

As the elevator landed on the C-Suite, Josh got ready to sprint out.

Almost there.

Upon the elevator's arrival ding, Joshua sprinted through the barely open doors.

♡ ♡ ♡

Lucas caressed his five o'clock shadow then readjusted his Bulgari luxury sunglasses that paired effortlessly with his Versace suit. He sat in the company helicopter with two gorgeous women as they clinked glasses of champagne.

As the helicopter sat itself down on top of the Double Digits headquarters, Lucas tried to decide between the athletic, bodybuilding blonde or the soft and curvy raven-haired delight. *I think I'll have both.*

Lucas kissed each woman sensually on the lips.

"Sir, I'm supposed to remind you of the time," the pilot said over the roar of the machine.

"Right," Lucas hollered back. He smiled at the women seductively. "Gotta run, ladies. Until tonight."

He put down his champagne flute and jumped out of the helicopter like a celebrity arriving to the red carpet. He looked at his gold watch, realized the time, and sprinted across the pad to the door, racing through it.

Fuck. Josh is gonna beat me.

Lucas raced down the steel, rickety rooftop stairs and burst through the stairwell door in a dead sprint to Pappy's office.

Almost there.

As Lucas reached the elevator, the steel doors chimed open and out raced Joshua in a sleek dark gray suit, getting two steps ahead of him.

"That's right, little brother," Josh laughed as he took the lead.

"Damn it!"

Lucas picked up the pace and just before they raced through Pappy's office door Lucas football-shoved Joshua to the side and dashed through the door.

"Not today, loser!" Lucas cackled.

Lucas burst into Pappy's office with his hands held above his head.

"I won, Paps." Lucas grinned as he fixed his tie and straightened himself up properly upon the observant stare of his very particular grandfather. "How the hell are ya today, old man?"

Lucas wrapped his arms around the gray-haired tiger and slapped him on the back.

"Lucas!" Paps bellowed, returning the squeeze. "My favorite youngest grandson. "How the hell are ya, kid?"

"Better than Josh." Lucas smirked as he let go and stepped back.

"What the hell is that nonsense on your face, Lucas?"

Lucas touched the scruff, then smiled. "The ladies like it."

"You know better."

"Yes, sir," Lucas said. He headed to the bathroom but stopped on a dime when he saw Alex.

"Alex." He nodded.

"Lucas."

What the hell is he doing here?

Lucas ran into the executive washroom and quickly returned with an electric shaver that was glued to his face. He sat down on the leather couch in front of Pappy's desk, taking up as much space as he could as Josh limped in. He held the latest magazine in one hand while rubbing his arm with the other.

"Cheaters never win, asshole," Josh smirked.

"On the contrary, we win all the time." Lucas gave him a wink as he shut off the razor and rubbed his now-smooth face. "Is it really cheating though? Or just excellent defense?"

"Bite me." Josh ignored Lucas in favor of a quick glance to the black and white picture of his grandparents on Pappy's desk. *He was always so close to Grandma.*

"Paps," Lucas hollered. He pointed to his face. "Good, right?"

"Better." Paps gave him a warning look. *I know what that means. Don't show up with scruff again.*

Joshua finally spied Alex on the other leather couch putting together paperwork. Alex dropped it in his briefcase as Josh straightened his tie and smoothed down his suit.

"Alex."

Josh nodded and extended his hand to Alex, who took it warmly.

"Josh."

They let go as Josh asked, "What are you—"

Paps interrupted as he grabbed Josh's shoulders with a loving shake. "My favorite oldest grandson." *He's totally trying to distract us both that Alex is here.*

Alex grabbed his briefcase to leave and gave a nod. "Paps."

"Later, buddy," Lucas said.

Lucas grabbed some of the candy in the delicate bowl on the glass table in front of him as Alex walked away.

"Yep," Alex said.

Alex threw his hand up and walked briskly out the door.

Lucas tossed a couple pieces of candy into his mouth and chomped wildly, enjoying every second of the delicious, chewy delight. He eyed Josh as Josh watched Alex leave. *He's wondering the same thing I am.*

"Why was Alex here?" Josh asked as he turned back to Paps.

"Don't you worry about it," Paps said.

Josh eyed Paps for a second. "You feelin' okay, Paps?"

Lucas had noticed that, too. Paps had seemed a little…off. *Pale, maybe? Slow? Something.*

"Best shape of my life," he retorted.

Paps slapped Joshua on the arm.

"Magazine cover is beautiful," Joshua said. He dropped it by the candy bowl. Josh looked at the candy then at Lucas gnawing on it and shook his head. Lucas flipped him off before Paps could see. "It's definitely more modern. Simple. Looks good. You do this?"

"You like that, huh?" Paps asked. He wiggled his gray eyebrows.

"I do," Josh said. "A step in the right direction to bring us a younger audience.

More contemporary. I like the cross-referencing of digital with print. QR codes. Social. All good."

Paps smiled, then stopped for a moment and looked them both over with a critical eye. Lucas felt the stare and straightened up a bit in his seat until Pappy's stare landed on Josh.

"Tie's a little out of place, Josh," Paps said. "Better stop letting your little brother kick your ass."

"Ahahahaha!" Lucas cackled as he pointed at Pappy, who shot back the same pointed finger with joy.

Josh retorted, "Okay, alright. He did *not* kick my ass."

Joshua straightened his tie.

Pappy said, "Tie said otherwise."

Paps tapped the magazine Josh dropped. "This is all Scout."

"Scout?" Joshua and Lucas asked at the same time.

Paps grinned.

"Get your ass up, Lucas," Paps snarled. "Walk with me, boys."

Paps cut a beeline for the door as Lucas gave Josh a raised eyebrow. Josh rewarded him with one in return.

We're both so used to this.

Whatever Paps had up his sleeve, Lucas was certain it had to do with him and Josh. And it likely was going to be a pain in the ass for both of them.

I'm certain of that.

3

Say Thank You

Scout walked through the hallways of Double Digits carrying her and Belle's coffees while skillfully dodging bustling on comers.

"Whoa," she said as she quickly navigated a rushing model. The woman's hair was awry in beauty clips, and she wore an overabundance of hot pink glitter eyeshadow and black eyeliner.

"Sorry," the five-foot, eleven-inch beauty said sweetly.

"No problem," Scout yelled over her shoulder. Scout was too short for modeling, even though her wickedly green eyes and exotic looks made her stand out. She could thank her mother for that, as well as for her size twelve hips.

"Sorry," she yelled again as she dodged another glamazon. They were all here for the next magazine shoot. So far, she approved.

The women were comprised of all shapes, sizes, and colors. They were dressed beautifully in the company's clothing, of which three of the fashion lines in this issue were courtesy of a trio of hot, new designers.

Scout's Honor was her favorite line, and not just because it had her name in it. The designer was sheik, understood the market, and was just a stunning human being. Paps had also taken a liking to her because she was so down-to-earth.

Scout stopped and peered into the dressing room. The models were being fitted before being shuffled over to hair and make-up. One of the make-up artists spied her and waved her over with a wide smile.

"Oh my God, the magazine cover is gorgeous," said Elise, a bright-eyed, platinum blonde with a pixie haircut to match her tiny frame. "You did so great giving Pappy direction on it. We all think you kicked ass. *Finally.* Someone who knows the audience and has the vision to move this company into the future."

Scout could feel the heat sliding across her cheeks as everyone in the room nodded at her.

"Thanks, Elise," Scout said. She gave a little shrug to show her appreciation. "Paps is so fantastic to work with. He's so, so smart. And he really appreciates his customers. You know he built this place for his wife? Plus, the model on the cover just made the clothes look fantastic. Beautiful."

"So are you," Elise said. "And t.b.h., stop giving everyone else credit. Just say thank you and move on. Take the credit you deserve."

That was something Scout's mother had told her many, many times, as a matter of gender equality and practicality.

"No one knows what women do because women don't ever say it," her mother had said. She was a professor at U.C. Berkley and held a doctorate in women's studies. "So, speak up, Scout."

Scout understood what her mother, who performed gender bias research as part of her teaching gig, was telling her. And Scout had no problem giving herself those kinds of compliments in private. But she just couldn't get past the idea that it took a team of people to make things happen, not just her. So, compliments bestowed on her that recognized only her efforts were hard to take.

Really hard.

"You know what, let me give you a quick makeover," Elise said. Her face lit with excitement. "Take five minutes. You have sooooo earned it."

"Oh, I have to get this coffee back to Belle," Scout hesitated. "She brought me cookies."

"I promise. I'll be fast. Here, sit."

Elise slapped the beauty chair. Scout knew she wasn't getting away without a new face.

"Okay but make it quick." Scout sat down in a rush as a stylist brought over an exquisite dress from the latest Scout's Honor line and took the coffee from her hands.

"This will be beautiful on you," the stylist said.

"Oh my." Scout smiled and fingered the expensive clothing. *Maybe just this once.* She rested her eyes and let them take care of her for a few blissful minutes.

4

Knuckleheads

As the three men walked through the clothing company and all its different areas, several of the women swooned for the attention of the two handsome grandsons.

Josh didn't mind the attention. A couple of them were cute, too. Maybe a little plump, but attractive. He was less concerned about their size and more concerned that some of them were just setting their sights on him and his brother because they were the heir apparents to Pappy's company.

Always hard to tell which ones are for real and which ones aren't.

Josh smiled at Paps as the older statesman shook hands and had conversations like a politician. If there had been a baby in the crowd, Paps would have picked it up and taken a photo with it.

His grandfather was tough but kind and had earned the respect of his employees. It was something Josh admired in Paps and desperately wanted for himself. He was getting there. He could tell that the employees were slowly warming up to him and Lucas.

"A couple things for you two knuckleheads," Paps said. He finally turned his attention back to the boys, talking to them over his shoulder as he led the way through the halls. "So, pay attention."

Just then, one of the women in the hallway caught Joshua's eye. He couldn't help but smile back at the short-haired beauty, her dark eyes sparkling, before he doubled over in pain thanks to a gut punch from Lucas. While Josh was bent over, Lucas shoved past him and started talking to the girl.

Paps was blissfully unaware of the antics behind him as he kept walking.

Joshua stood up with pursed lips and knocked the back of Lucas's leg as it buckled. The girl lost interest in both men as Lucas dropped to his knee.

"I'm thinking about bringing Scout on in a much larger role," Paps said over his shoulder. "Dropping her contract and making her an employee."

Josh snapped his attention to Paps. "Wait, what? I thought she was just advising you on trends and creative?"

Pappy kept walking as Lucas shoved Joshua.

"She's proven to be much more astute than originally expected," Paps said over his shoulder.

Joshua shoved Lucas back, then raced to catch up with Pappy.

"Paps. You can't be serious," Josh said. "We don't even know her."

Pappy looked back at the two with an eyebrow raise as they each straightened up.

"I am serious, Josh. And I think you'll agree with me once you get to know her." Paps gave Josh a little wink that put Josh on notice about Scout. *What is Paps doing?*

Paps and Josh shared a long, suspicious stare before Paps looked the boys up and down and eyed their mussed-up clothes. They each straightened their ties and suits and smoothed them down. Paps finally nodded and started walking again.

"Scout has been here a few months, not that you two noticed or cared, when you should have," said Paps with deep disapproval. "She has a background in fashion and business. Smart girl. Creative. And more importantly, she gets our audience."

Pappy glanced back at Josh.

"We get our audience, too," Josh said. He smoothed his clothing.

"Yeah, big girls wanna feel hot," Lucas said dryly. He straightened his tie.

Joshua and Paps faced him with questioning faces.

"No...," Josh uttered. He gave Lucas a "wtf" look. Lucas shrugged. "Women want to feel beautiful. All women. Period."

Lucas rolled his eyes. "I literally said the same thing."

Pappy shook his head at them both, then turned and started walking again.

Joshua looked at Lucas. "What the fuck is wrong with you?" he asked.

"What? I'm not wrong. I'm just not gonna sugar-coat everything like you do."

They followed Paps as they walked past a meeting room with beautiful plus-sized models getting fitted. Lucas glanced in and they smiled at him. He stopped and smiled back.

Joshua grabbed him and pulled him forward. They moved quickly down the hallway.

"So, wait, what are you hoping for Scout to do? What role?" Josh asked.

"We'll see," Paps said. He shrugged. "She helped art direct the cover for this most recent magazine. The one you love. The one you said is moving in the right direction. She's got an eye for visuals and a business acumen beyond her years."

"Lucas and I are supposed to be taking over that aspect of the company over," Josh said annoyed. "I wanna meet this Scout."

"I'll make sure you meet her soon," Paps said. "Give me a week or so. We can go have lunch. Take her to Primanti Brothers. A proper welcome to Pittsburgh." He gave Josh a mischievous look over his shoulder.

*There it is again. What is his deal with me
and this Scout girl?*

Joshua moved to get ahead of Paps at the corner.

"Okay. When next week?" Josh demanded. He stepped into the hallway and turned to face Paps. As he did, Scout rounded the corner at the same time and *SLAM.*

Josh yelped and jumped back as he pulled on his shirt to keep the hot coffee off his skin.

"Oh my God, I'm so sorry," Scout said apologetically. Flustered, she dropped the coffees on the ground and pulled at his shirt to keep the blistering liquid from burning him.

"I got it," Josh said calmly. He lightly took hold of her wrists and gave her a slight smile. "It's okay. Really. I've got it."

He let go of her with a patient nod. He glanced down at his formerly fresh white shirt and beautiful suit that were now covered in coffee and cream.

He finally looked at the young woman and was instantly captivated by her green eyes. *Oh my.*

His insides turned to molten lava as he took in the sleek burgundy dress hugging her sexy curves, the heels that gave shape to her calves, the long, rich brown hair that fell at her ample breasts, and the pouty, perfect Cabernet lips he wanted to chew on. *Chew on? Pull yourself together, man.*

"I didn't...I'm...," Scout stuttered. A flush of embarrassment brought color to her cheeks. He could see she was mortified as she glanced between the three men. *God, she's beautiful. And those exotic, green eyes. Good Lord.*

"It's okay," Josh finally got out. He could hear Paps and Lucas laughing as Joshua pursed his lips. He took a step away from the coffee puddle on the floor.

A few employees started bringing over clothes and cleaning up.

Paps smiled broadly. "Josh, *this* is Scout."

She half-smiled, half-cringed as Joshua flicked his eyes toward her with a sigh and a grin.

Of course this is Scout.

And now he started to suspect why Paps had given him the eye about her.

Not only was she apparently smart and good for the company, but Josh suddenly guessed that Paps had ideas she might be interesting to Josh as well.

Paps might be right about that.

One thing was certain, Josh couldn't ignore the way his heart beat a little bit faster at the sight of her. And more importantly, he didn't want to ignore it, either.

5

Excuse My Missing Shirt

Scout walked into Pappy's office carrying a new, white dress shirt and tie. She quickly found herself watching Lucas's intense stare as he attempted to beat Pappy in a tightly contested chess match.

"Bathroom," the patriarch said without looking up. He pointed across the office as he and Lucas stared with competitive concentration at the beautifully sculpted pieces on the glass chess table.

Scout shook her head with a grin and walked to the executive bathroom door. As she started to gently knock, Joshua swung it open. She caught her breath at his shirtless, damp chest.

"Oh," she gasped.

She swallowed hard as her eyes met his, her lips slightly parting. Without actively telling her body to do so, it leaned, almost magnetically, toward him.

His body responded in kind, and he held her stare as his eyes softened at the corners. His lips opened slightly as she heard a low breath escape from his throat.

"Josh! Hurry up," Lucas shouted. "Paps has news for us."

At the sound of Lucas's voice, she and Josh reacted as if a spell had been broken.

"Oh, umm, uh...shirt. Your shirt. Here ya go." Scout recovered first and quickly handed it to him.

Joshua shook his head as though clearing it, took the shirt, and put it on with a slight laugh.

"Thank you," he said. He gave her a humorous grin. "I hope you'll excuse my missing shirt. Someone spilled coffee on it."

She chuckled as she tried hard not to glance at his chest. It was a firm wonderland of manicured chest hair and muscle. *Stop that!*

She struggled to maintain her decorum as he buttoned the crisp fabric and tucked it in.

"It's okay," she countered. She leaned against the door frame. "I've seen you naked before."

He jolted to attention as she laughed.

"Paps. He told me about a wasp incident?" She raised a curious eyebrow. "He showed me a picture of you in the bathtub. Age five, I believe."

Josh laughed and said, "Ahh, the wasp sting picture."

"Yep. It's in his top desk drawer."

"Yeah, he loves to embarrass me with that. I was quite…swollen…in that picture."

She chuckled at his humor.

"From the wasp stings." Josh winked at her.

"Yeah, I noticed. Must have hurt."

"Not nearly as much as my pride. Did he tell you the whole story?"

Scout shook her head. "He said to just tell you I'd seen you naked, and you would tell me the rest."

He finished putting his shirt together.

"Sounds like Pap," Josh said. He turned his full attention to her with a warm grin. She couldn't help but notice the rich, dark brown color of his eyes and the way they sparkled with humor.

"I fell off my horse into a wasp nest," said Josh matter of fact. "After they finished me off, I landed myself in a tub full of warm water and baking soda, thanks to Paps."

"Ahh. And what made you fall off the horse in the first place?"

Josh held her stare for a second too long before he answered. "A pretty girl."

Scout's heart skipped a beat at his enveloping gaze. "Pretty girls have a way of making men fall off their horses."

"Yeah," he said. "They do."

They stood quietly as a noticeable heat passed between them. Finally, Josh spoke.

"Perfect fit."

She nodded as he held her stare.

"Yeah..." she mumbled.

"The shirt," he quipped.

She snapped out of it.

"Oh," she said. "Yes. Yeah."

"How'd you know my size?" he asked.

"Oh, uh, fashion degree. I went to the Columbus College of Art & Design in Columbus. Ohio," she clarified as she stood straight. "Design and marketing. I know...clothes. Sizes. How to market them. All the things."

She held up the tie in her hand as he grinned at her.

"Your tie," she said.

As he moved to take it, Scout stepped to him to put it around his neck.

"Oh, sorry," he said confused.

"Oh, no, me, *I'm* sorry," she babbled. "You're a grown...grown man. You can put on your own tie."

She laughed awkwardly as she plopped the tie playfully against his chest and tried not to notice how deliciously solid it was. An electric spark zapped between them when he brushed her fingers to take it.

"Ow," they both said at the same time.

"Must be the fabric and the carpet," she said breathlessly.

"Yeah. Must be," he said.

They shared a goofy, awkward grin before he firmly took the tie and stepped in front of the bathroom mirror to adjust it. She rolled her eyes at herself and shook her head.

"Good tie," he said.

"Thanks."

"You do know clothes," he complimented. She could tell by his tone that he appreciated that about her.

"I really do. It's a passion," she said.

He stepped out of the bathroom, clicking off the light, and stood right in front of her as a palpable tension affected them both.

"Are you also one of our models?" he asked.

"What? Oh...," she mumbled. She'd forgotten about her mini-makeover earlier and smoothed down her hair and dress at his gaze.

"No, no, no. I'm friends with the stylists and hair and make-up," she said clumsily. "They liked the cover, so they wanted to do something nice for me."

"It was a beautiful issue," he said. "And this dress...it makes your eyes stand out."

"Thank you," she said quietly. She caught her breath at the sultry look in his eyes.

They drank each other in for a sizzling moment.

"I should...," he started. He pointed to Paps and Lucas.

She realized she was blocking his path out of the bathroom.

"Oh, yeah. Sure. I'm sorry," she stammered. She stepped out of his way. "I have work to do."

Joshua smiled and walked past her toward Paps. *God, he smells good, too.*

He stopped and turned back to her as though he heard what she said.

Oh my God, did I say that out loud?

"You could be, you know."

"Could be what?" she asked, relieved her thoughts were *not* tumbling out of her mouth uninvited.

"One of our models," he said with a grin.

He swaggered away to sit with Paps and Lucas.

She knew she was practically glowing as she walked out of the office.

She floated back to her desk, sat down, and sighed. Her smile was wide as she breathed slowly, her eyes heavy with happiness.

Belle walked in and looked her over.

"What's the matter with you? Didn't you hear me saying your name?" Belle asked curiously.

"Huh?" Scout asked.

"Why do you look like that? Your expression. That dress. The make-up." Belle pressed on as she investigated Scout's desk and hands. "And where's the coffee?"

"It's just...a beautiful day," Scout said. Then she realized what Belle was asking. "Oh, Belle, the coffee! I'm sorry. I had a bit of an accident. I'll go back for a new one."

Scout stood quickly but Belle put a hand up to stop her.

"That can wait. Your cell phone almost vibrated off your desk about fifteen minutes ago. California number."

"What?"

Scout snapped out of it as she grabbed her phone and listened to the voicemail.

I can't believe it.

"What is it?" Belle asked.

"Just a really inspired telemarketer," Scout said coolly.

"Harumph," Belle uttered suspiciously as she walked back to her desk. "When you're ready to tell me what's really going on, you know where to find me."

Belle was right to be skeptical. It was *not* a telemarketer. It was StudioX. Their main competitor.

According to the company's COO, they'd seen her work and wanted to talk. Scout wasn't sure about taking that call. First, she loved working here and, second, Paps had alluded to extending her contract or maybe transforming it into an employee situation.

And, well, Josh.

Oh, come on...you just met Josh.

She smiled at the thought of him. Then shook it away just as quickly.

Working for a company like StudioX could completely transform her career and its trajectory. She at least had to consider it. Right?

I'll call them back later. I just need a minute to think.

And before she knew it, she *was* thinking again.

About Josh. And those rich dark eyes that she already knew she was getting lost in.

6

Checkmate

Joshua sat down next to Lucas just as Paps said with cocky confidence, "Checkmate."

"No!" Lucas shouted. He jumped up and slapped at the air. "Paps. Damn it."

"You haven't beat me yet, kid." Paps stood up with a satisfied grin and buttoned his jacket before smoothing out his tie.

"It's comin', Paps," Lucas said. He grabbed some candy out of the bowl and shoved it in his mouth. "I can feel it."

"Whatever you say," Paps said. He shook his head as he stuffed his hands in his pockets and leaned against his desk.

Josh grinned as he fiddled with his tie. His mind drifted to Scout and her perfectly painted lips. They did this thing where they curled up at the corners when she was deep in thought.

"Josh?"

"Huh?" Josh peered at his grandfather.

Pappy tried unsuccessfully to hide a grin. "Who ya thinkin' about, kid?"

"No one." Josh shook his head and tucked away his smile. "Alright. What's going on, Paps?"

Paps grinned like a Cheshire cat. "I'm retiring early, boys."

"Wait, what?" Lucas asked. He dumped the candy in his hand back in the bowl.

"Paps." Josh just shook his head at the patriarch. "You're kidding, right?"

"I'm not," he said. "It's time. And the quandary is—I don't know which one of you to leave the company to. So, I've decided, you're gonna do what the two of you do best: you're gonna compete for it."

"What?" they asked at the same time.

Lucas flung his hands in the air and looked directly at Josh. "I mean. I love ya, Josh, but come on." He turned to Paps. "I've given you the healthiest bottom line this company has ever seen. And that's after Josh put you in the red."

"We *had* to go in the red to invest in digital and creative assets." Josh countered. "That's part of the modernization I've brought to the table."

He turned to Lucas and shook his head. "Easy to put the plane in the air after I built the runway, little brother."

"Gi'me a break," Lucas huffed.

Josh turned back to Paps. "Everything from enhanced user experience across digital properties to making it easier for customers to both buy and receive their purchases. You couldn't have that healthy bottom line without me."

Joshua flicked a challenging eyebrow at Lucas. "You're fucking welcome."

Lucas shook his head and laughed.

"None of that matters unless you get the deals done, brother," said Lucas. "Gotta have the relationships and sales. So, *you're* fucking welcome."

Pappy stood and jerked his hands into a stopping motion. "Okay, enough. You're both right."

Josh locked eyes with Lucas. *Asshole.* Lucas mouthed to him, "Asshole."

At least we're on the same page.

They looked back to Paps.

"And now you see my problem," he said. "You could both run this thing as CEO with the other taking a COO or CFO position. But you both want it, am I right? Both of you want to be CEO?"

Joshua and Lucas glared at each other, looked back to Paps, and both nodded.

"Then let the games begin," Paps said. He leaned back against the desk with a satisfied grin.

"Here's the deal. You have seven days beginning forty-eight hours from right now to meet with seven plus-sized women. All of whom have a connection to this company."

Joshua sighed and stuffed his hands in his pockets as Lucas grabbed a handful of candy from the bowl and started chomping on it.

"Seven women because there are seven major plus-sized stereotypes, according to me, that I've noticed your father putting in your heads since you were in middle school," he said. He crossed his arms. "Stereotypes that I feel are clouding your judgment about this company and what we stand for."

"For Josh maybe," said Lucas. He gave a Maverick grin. "I'm an equal opportunity womanizer."

"You would say something like that,"
Josh smirked. "Jackass."

"Shut up. Both of you," Paps ordered.
"Bottom-line: Neither of you has ever—" he
looked straight at Lucas— "*seriously* dated a
plus-sized woman or even, really, spent time
with one professionally or otherwise, except
for my Bessie. Your beloved grandmother,
God rest her soul. And since you haven't,
what the hell could either of you skirt
chasers know about what these women
really need?"

Lucas piped up. "I mean—"

"It's a rhetorical question, Lucas," Paps
interrupted with annoyance. "The answer is
nothing. You don't know anything."

"What are the stereotypes?" Josh
interrupted.

"Well, based on what I've seen from your
father and the way he's talked about women
to the two of you, he's put in your heads that

they're lazy and unmotivated, that they're dirty and unkempt—ridiculous."

Paps shook his head.

"That they want to be that way, that they're insecure and don't date, which, clearly that's not true."

Paps waved his hand at Lucas, who smiled like a champ.

"Mmm, Stacey," Lucas murmured. "And Denise. And Jennifer." He flicked a wicked grin and eye raise at Josh, who sneered back.

"Over here, boys." They turned back to Paps. "There's also this idea that they have nicer personalities because they have to and, well, that they're just plain not healthy."

Paps stood up and eyed the photo of him and Bessie before turning back to the boys.

"Listen, maybe I'm wrong, here." He shrugged. "Maybe you two haven't listened to your father as closely as I suspect. I don't know. But this is my damn company. And Bessie was my world."

Joshua played with his tie and sighed as he gave his grandfather a once over. *He looks tired.*

"This company was a tribute to her and her struggles," Paps said quietly. "So, this choice *has* to be right. And unbiased. So, I'm not going to decide."

Paps flared his hands out with an affirmative nod.

"The women will decide."

"What now?" Josh asked with surprise.

"Yes!" Lucas jogged around the couch and came back to a stop where he started.

"You heard me." He nodded with confidence. "Women are intuitive creatures. They'll know which one of you is bullshitting them and which one isn't. They'll *know* who gets it. So, here's how this is gonna go down."

Josh and Lucas glanced at each other competitively before turning their attention back to Paps. *Of course. Of course Paps is doing this.*

"Alex and I will select the women and he'll set up brief meetings with them. And then, well, it gets a little Survivor-like," Paps said. He walked over to his bar cart and poured a whiskey neat. "Every woman gets a vote for either you, Josh, or you, Lucas."

He took a swig of his drink and enjoyed it with a smile.

"Each of the first six women will vote. If one of you gets four votes, it's over, the seventh woman won't vote. She'll only act as a witness to your meetings, and she'll capture their votes. But…" he eyed them with a smile. "If there's a tie, the seventh woman *will* vote. And whomever she chooses will take over as CEO and run the company."

They both stared blankly at Paps. *Unbelievable.*

Lucas asked, "What are the rules?"

"You can't talk business with these women. You can't sleep with them."

Paps looked directly at Lucas. Lucas smiled proudly while Josh shook his head.

"You can't meet with the women outside of the arranged time and place. You can't tell anyone outside this room, with the exception of Alex, what's going on. Not even the seventh woman—she doesn't even know what these women are voting on or that she's the final vote. I want her to hear and see everything objectively."

Paps took a final swig and put his empty glass down. "Do we have a deal?"

Lucas smiled and extended his hand as Paps took it.

Lucas said, "Deal."

"Joshua?" Paps asked as he let go of Lucas's hand. Paps raised a questioning eyebrow.

Joshua thought for a second.

Josh asked, "What's the seventh stereotype? You only gave us six."

"That plus-sized women are just plain unattractive."

Josh asked, "And, who's the seventh woman? The tiebreaker."

Paps shoved his hands in his pockets with a triumphant grin.

7

The Tiebreaker

Scout sat at her desk and stared awkwardly at her two visitors as they towered over her.

She asked, "Is there something I can help you both with?"

Joshua and Lucas smiled at Scout as they stood in front of her. Joshua with his arms crossed and Lucas with one hand shoved in his pocket and the other filled with candy that he was pilfering into his mouth.

Lucas said, "Just...wanted to say hi and it was so nice to meet you today when you threw steaming hot coffee all over my brother."

"Oh." Scout could feel a warm heat of embarrassment rise in her cheeks.

"Speaking of," Josh said. "Thank you again for the shirt."

Joshua smiled as their eyes met. Scout could feel the intensity of the heat in her face continue to rise. *Why is he so handsome? Why am I suddenly noticing?*

Her breath skipped as she dipped her eyes down and tucked a hair behind her ear before turning back to his sultry stare.

She could feel Lucas's eyes on her as he slapped her desk to get her attention. Startled, she flipped a glance back to the younger brother.

"Sorry," he said. He flashed his pearly whites. "So, heard the magazine cover was your handiwork. Really...beautiful."

Lucas tried to catch her eye with his Casanova moves, but she wasn't falling for it. She crinkled her forehead at him. "Thanks."

She turned back to Josh with a questioning stare. Neither of these two had noticed her until just this morning and now they were at her desk?

Josh said, "Well, we better get going. Sorry for the interruption. Just wanted to say congrats on the cover. Again, beautiful."

Joshua smiled at her, and she could barely contain the joy in her gut at his attention. She knew the chemistry between them was palpable as she glanced at Lucas and saw his frown. *Why does he care?*

Lucas slapped Joshua's arm. "Let's go, eh."

"Yeah," Josh said.

She hated that he finally broke eye contact with her.

"Okay," she said. She gave Joshua a sexy grin as the brothers turned and walked out of her office toward the private elevator.

That was weird.

Something *is* up. But what does it have to do with me?

♥ ♥ ♥

Joshua and Lucas stepped into the private elevator and hit the only button available to push, which led to the private parking floor.

Joshua was half-smiling and smug. He glanced at Lucas who was smirking and annoyed. Lucas turned to Joshua. When he did, Joshua turned to face him.

Lucas said, "Okay, quit with the gloating. You have an advantage with Scout. So…we make a deal."

"Fine," Josh said. He sighed and crossed his arms. "Your proposal?"

"Okay, I won't sleep with any of the women or contact them outside of the meetings, which, we both knew I was going to do anyway."

Lucas ran his fingers down his silky tie with a cheeky smile as Josh nodded.

"Right," Josh agreed. "And I won't use Scout's...flirting...to my very clear advantage."

Lucas made a questioning face.

"What?" Josh asked.

Lucas half-smiled as the elevator doors dinged open.

"What?" Josh asked again, more annoyed this time.

Joshua followed Lucas into the garage.

Lucas said, "*Her* flirting?"

Lucas turned around and stopped as Joshua halted in front of him. Joshua put his hands in his pockets, glanced around, and then looked back to Lucas with a smile.

"She's not my type."

Lucas smirked with a nod and walked away chuckling.

"She *is* your type. You just don't know it yet."

Joshua followed with a shake of his head as Lucas walked to his Lamborghini and opened it.

Josh said, "I think I know my type."

Lucas shook his head as he faced his brother.

"Look, I'm gonna break this down for you," Lucas said, using his hands to emphasize what he meant. "We both love the women. But, unlike you, I love all shapes and sizes and colors and attitudes of the fairer sex. Yes, please. To all of them. Dear God, they smell so good. They're like a field of flowers—"

"Lucas!" Josh interrupted.

"Right," he said. "But you and Dad? You both have such a narrow way of thinking about women. It's why you shouldn't run the company, Josh."

Lucas stopped playing around and got serious.

"You're older. You're amazing at *pretending* to understand our customer," Lucas said. "But you don't. Not really."

Josh put up a hand to stop him and said, "I know—"

"No, you don't," Lucas interrupted. "So...I'll do this competition because that's what Paps wants. And I'll play fair, because I made that deal with you and you're my brother."

Josh exhaled a deep sigh as he crossed his arms.

"But make no mistake, Josh. I don't think you should run it," said Lucas. "And not just because you don't know the audience. You don't know yourself. You've spent your life doing what Dad wants, doing what Paps wants...do you even know what the hell *you* want? You're playing dress-up, man. And *that* is why you shouldn't have the company."

Josh uncrossed his arms and rubbed his face with his hands before throwing them to his sides and stepping to Lucas.

"At least I don't act like a privileged asshole with ridiculous cars, arriving by helicopters, threesomes and orgies and acting like a dick," Josh spat. "You think Paps wants that as the face of his company? Dragging his name and this company through the mud? Your stupid antics are like a five-year-old's. Grow up."

"Why, so I can be just like you?" Lucas asked. "No, thanks. At least I'm real."

"You're a child," Josh sneered.

"No, *you're* a child."

Lucas shoved Josh. Josh shoved him back. They eyed each other for a second before Joshua turned and walked away as Lucas got in his car.

Two seconds later, Joshua walked back as Lucas got out of the car and walked toward him.

Josh asked, "Are you going to Dad's for dinner?"

"Yeah."

"Text me their new address."

Lucas texted it as Joshua's phone lit up.

Lucas said, "I need some cash. Helicopter can't stop at an ATM."

Joshua pulled out his wallet and handed him cash from inside it.

"Asshole," Josh muttered under his breath as he put his wallet away.

"Dick," Lucas said as he pulled out his wallet and put the cash in. They eyed each other briefly as Lucas put his wallet away.

They each shook their heads, then walked their separate ways as Josh shoved his hands in his pockets. He let out a huff of air as his mind flashed back to Scout and the attraction in her eyes when she saw him shirtless.

She had tried to put his tie on for him. It was a sexy little move he would have allowed if it weren't for the fact that Paps wanted to hire her as an employee. And if she was an employee and he was the CEO, she'd be his subordinate.

Best to stop thinking about her. And how she smelled like the most intoxicating mix of amber and vanilla ever created.

Josh paused and shook away the thought of her as he reached for the driver's side door of his Jeep. Not thinking about Scout in "that way" might prove to be the hardest part of this whole competition.

Or maybe it would be the fact that there was something to what Lucas had said.

And if I lose the company, what will I do then?

8

He's Gone

After twenty minutes of driving, Josh pulled up to a large, contemporary farmhouse just outside of Pittsburgh's downtown core. It was located in the Fox Chapel area, known for housing some of the wealthiest families in the area, including theirs. They were on the outskirts of it and owned a significant chunk of land.

The house that Pappy had bought and renovated was a simple structure with a stunning wraparound porch, both of which betrayed the lavish luxury within.

Paps had bought this place after his first big financial year at Double Digits, and it had stayed in the family since then, operating as a sort of timeshare among them.

Josh's favorite part of the peaceful property was the large pond the house overlooked and the several acres of beautifully kept terrain that cocooned it all.

Of all the spaces he occupied regularly, including his downtown condo, this was the one he felt the most connected to. He'd always wondered why that was and had never really landed on a complete answer.

The house was amazing, sure, with a blend of country and opulence that was unparalleled in real estate circles. And the surrounding nature made the city feel further away than it really was, which gave it the illusion of an escape.

It could also be that his mother's ashes were spread here. Josh, his father, and Lucas, had walked the property the day after her remains were delivered and let the sacred dust surf the wind to whatever destination she wanted to go.

I wonder where she landed.

She would have loved the idea of riding the wind to wherever it took her. She had been a wild, free spirit. So different from his father, who was much more severe and grounded. "Balanced" is the way Paps had described the two lovebirds. "Yin and yang," Paps had said.

Josh had been only eight years old when she died. Lucas was six. The drunk driver who slammed into his mother's car on her way home from the art gallery she owned had gotten out of prison years ago, but the prison he and Lucas lived in still felt very real.

"Miss you Mom," he whispered. Josh pulled the keys out of the ignition and stepped out of his Jeep, slamming the door behind him.

The late afternoon sun was beginning to set, and the golden hour glow was upon him. It made the property look like a postcard.

Maybe it's the pond I'm drawn to.

The pond. Just before she had died, his mother, Anastasia, had taken him down to the still body of water at golden hour and set up an easel for herself and a tiny one for him. She had given him a brush from her paint-splashed canvas bag and then plopped some paint on a paper plate and said, "Go to town."

"What town?" he had asked. She had laughed when he did. She had a large, unencumbered laugh that had rung his ears with joy.

"I meant, just do whatever you want," she'd said as she had cupped his face lovingly.

They'd stood there together and splashed colors against canvas until twilight had fully set in. She had painted the sky and all its colors, but Josh had chosen to paint the tall, swaying weeds that lined the algae-laden pond.

"Why did you paint those old things?" she had asked.

"They remind me of you," he had answered.

It's the only conversation with his mother he remembered. The only words he ever remembered saying to her, except, of course, I love you.

"What the hell?" Josh turned as a jungle green Jaguar pulled up next to him, the music so loud Josh could feel the bass thumping in his body. He looked over at Lucas, who was smiling and dancing behind the wheel. Josh tried to be annoyed, but he couldn't. He let out a chuckle. His little brother was a pain in his ass, but damn it, the kid was a bright light in a dark world.

"Why do you always drive the same, boring car?" Lucas chided as he jumped out of the Jag.

"Not sure. Why are you a douche who *never* drives the same car?" Josh said as he walked around the Jag.

Lucas laughed. "Because I can. Because it's fun. Ever heard o' that word before?"

"I have a word for ya," Josh said.

"I bet you do." Lucas slapped Josh's arm as the two met at the front of the car. "I'm hungry big brother. Let's eat."

Josh and Lucas walked along the cracked stone path to the front door as their father, R.J, in a button down and casual pants, and his long-time girlfriend, Katherine, in a long sweater over leather tights, walked out.

"Hey, boys," Katherine said.

Katherine could never replace his mother, but she was close. The fact that she never tried to act like their mother was probably what Josh respected most. What he respected second was that when he and Lucas had needed her over the years, she was there. Without question.

"Katherine," Josh said warmly as he enveloped her in a hug.

"How are ya, Josh?" she replied. She gave him a squeeze. When she pulled back, she shot him a questioning look. "You look like you've been thinkin'."

"Only you would notice that." He offered her a tired smile as R.J. and Lucas whooped it up after their bro hug. *Two peas in a pod.*

His father was a serious man but a playboy at heart, very much like Lucas. But unlike Lucas, their dad was extremely particular about everything, from how clean his house was to the size of his woman. And that was very much like Josh.

Josh had always thought the early death of his grandmother—R.J.'s mother,

Bessie—influenced that trait in his dad, but R.J. would never admit to such a thing.

"Josh," R.J. barked. He let go of Lucas and walked over to pull his oldest into a hug as Katherine headed for the youngest brother. "How the hell are you, son?"

"Good, dad," Josh said.

"You look good. Healthy," R.J. said. "Keep that up. You gettin' to the gym?"

"As much as I can," Josh said.

"Good. Keep your heart healthy," R.J. said. He tapped his chest.

"Enough of that," Katherine said. She let go of Lucas and walked up to Josh, looping her arm in his as she pulled him toward the house. R.J. and Lucas followed suit. "Let's enjoy a meal together, boys."

Josh appreciated that Katherine knew how to handle his father. Lord knows, Josh was still trying to figure the man out himself.

"Yeah," Josh echoed. "Let's eat."

♥ ♥ ♥

Josh noted the fresh spread of vegetables, the lean meats, the absence of dairy or sugar from their dinner table—except for the wine, of course. It was a beautiful spread, to be sure. And delicious. *But clinical.*

As the conversation turned from polite chit-chat to business, the boys gave each other competitive glances.

R.J. took the opportunity to once again pitch his company as a possibility for the boys to run. "I don't know why the hell neither of you want my chain of fitness centers?"

"I'm goin' where the real money is, dad, no offense," Lucas said.

"None taken," R.J. raised his glass to Lucas, then took a sip. "And you, Josh?"

"Just, uh…" Josh mumbled. He didn't know why he didn't want his father's empire of fitness centers that spanned the Midwest and east coast. If he was honest with himself, he wasn't entirely sure why he wanted Double Digits, except that he'd always wanted it. *I did always want it, right?* "It's not my thing, dad."

"Not your thing, pffft," R.J. groaned. He took a long sip of wine. "Plus-sized chicks aren't your thing."

"R.J.," Katherine chastised. "Don't talk like that."

"What? They're not," R.J. said defensively.

"I don't like it." Katherine clammed up, stabbing at her food and drinking her wine with an attitude.

Josh appreciated that about her. When she didn't like something, she said so. When R.J. pissed her off, she told him. And when it came to women, Katherine was a girl's girl. She appreciated women of all shapes and sizes, and she did *not* appreciate R.J.'s opposite take.

Josh cleared his throat to pull attention to him and give Katherine a breather.

"On another note, dad, have you noticed Paps seems a little..." he hesitated.

"Sick," Lucas finished.

"Somethin'." Josh agreed.

R.J. said, "Yeah, I saw that yesterday when he stopped by the gym. Tired, too. I'll call the old bastard tomorrow."

"Good," Josh said. He eyed his father and then it hit him. *Paps was at the gym?* "Wait, why was Paps at your fitness center?"

A little smirk on Katherine's face turned into a plucky smile as she glanced at R.J.

and took a sip of her wine. As she put it down, she asked, "Yes, R.J., why was that?"

Josh glanced between them as R.J. shot her a look that could kill.

"Paps…he volunteered my fitness center for a *Digits* magazine shoot for fitness gear." R.J. picked up his wine and chugged it.

Josh and Lucas glanced at each other and chuckled.

"So, your gym is gonna be flooded with gorgeous plus-sized women wearin' smokin' hot yoga pants?" Lucas asked with piqued interest. "Sign me up for that day."

"When's the shoot?" Josh asked.

"Couple weeks." R.J. shrugged. "Old bastard."

"I've never known you to bend so easily when it comes to your business," Josh said. "Especially where Paps is concerned."

R.J. shrugged. "Hey. Gets them in the gym. Maybe it'll inspire them to get in a workout."

"How do you know they don't workout already?" Katherine rebuked as a phone rang.

"Can we talk about somethin' else?" R.J. ate his food brusquely as he yanked vegetables off his fork with his teeth. The room was silent as the housemaid answered the phone on its third shrill vibrato.

She walked in just after and Josh quickly noticed the strange look on her face.

"Mr. Janssen?" she asked. R.J. turned to her.

"Yes?"

"There's an employee from Double Digits on the phone. Amber? She says it's an emergency."

"Amber?" R.J.'s face became immediately concerned as he walked to the next room and took the call.

When he came back to the table, Josh could already see it wasn't good. And when his father finally peered at him and Lucas, he already knew what had happened before R.J. spoke it into existence.

"Paps," he said. "He's gone."

9

Legal and Binding

Josh stood at the foot of Paps' grave and stared down at his grandpa's slate-gray casket. The sleek vessel was a stark contrast to the crumbling earth that surrounded it.

He raised his eyes and peered at hundreds upon hundreds of people exiting the cemetery. Some dabbed their eyes, some dashed to lunch, others scrolled on their cell phones. All of them were here to honor his grandfather.

I wonder where she is?

Josh knew Scout was here, but he tried to keep it under wraps that he was looking for her. It wouldn't be kosher. And yet…*is that her?*

The woman turned. *Nope.*

Scout and Paps had worked so closely together in these last few months. She had led him to a modernization of the brand that impressed Josh. Not only that, but Paps had indicated something in those last few interactions with him that Josh should get to know Scout. *And now I want to.*

"I should'a called him more," R.J. said abruptly from the other side of the grave.

"He knew you loved him," Josh replied. He looked around for Lucas. His little brother leaned against a tree a few feet away. Josh peered at him questioningly.

"You're uncharacteristically quiet."

"Yeah, well…" Lucas trailed off as his eyes took on a glossy sheen.

"Did, uh…did you two say good-bye?" R.J. asked.

Lucas gave a light nod as Josh answered. "Yeah…I guess. We were with him. That morning."

"You boys made his life worth living," R.J. said quietly. "You really made him proud, ya know? More than I ever did."

"He was proud of you, dad," Josh said.

R.J. shifted his weight. "Yeah, well, Alex is waiting for us at Pappy's office."

"He was with Paps the morning he died," Lucas said quietly.

"What for?" R.J. asked.

Josh and Lucas stole a questioning look at each other. They weren't supposed to tell anyone about the competition. Had that changed with Pappy's death?

"Somethin' about the will, I think," Josh answered as Lucas looked on. "Paps mentioned he might be retiring early."

"Harumph," R.J. grunted. "Well, I guess we better go find out."

Scout sat calmly in Pappy's office as she waited for everyone to arrive. She pulled a compact from her Chanel purse and double-checked her lipstick. She could tell Josh liked to stare at her lips, and this rich, warm burgundy was what she'd been wearing that day in Pappy's office. A smile crossed her face. *What is it about Josh?*

Her eyes scanned Pappy's office and landed on the black and white photo of him and Bessie. It felt more poignant than ever. Pappy's death was not just the end of an era, it was the end of a love story.

"Oh," she said quietly as tears rushed unexpectedly to her eyes. She stared at the ceiling and blinked them back, taking a deep breath and exhaling. *A beautiful love story.*

"Scout?"

She knew the voice before she turned and couldn't stop the bright bursts of excitement that hit her gut in response.

"Josh," she said lightly. She turned to face him. Behind him was Lucas, followed by R.J., whom she only knew from photos Paps had shown her.

"Why are you…" he trailed off. He looked confused and she was, too.

"I'm not sure," she said. She shrugged. "Alex texted me to be here."

"Oh," Josh said. He closed the distance between them slowly and cautiously. "Good to see you."

"You, too," she said quietly.

"Were you at the funeral?"

"I was. Towards the back. I thought it was better to let family and friends be close to Paps."

"As far as I can tell from what Paps said, you should have been much closer," Josh said. He smiled at her, and she felt the heat from it all the way down to her toes.

"Yeah, we did a lot of good work together the last few months," she said. She returned his smile, and his heat. For a moment, it felt like they were the only two standing there. Then…*something*. There was a flicker in his eyes like he remembered he shouldn't be so close. The moment turned cold as he stepped back from her and Lucas stepped up.

"Scout," Lucas said. He reached out his hand and she shook it. "Do you know why we're here?"

"I don't, I'm sorry."

R.J. followed right behind, offering his hand. "I've heard about you." She accepted and shook it.

"Paps was singing your praises," he continued. "Loved the magazine, too. You really nailed the look and feel."

"Thank you," she said.

"Hello, everyone." Alex breezed in with a briefcase. He was all business, as usual.

"Sorry for the short notice," he said. He sat down on the leather couch and put his briefcase on the table. "I'm sure you're all wondering why you're here."

As Alex began to talk, Scout felt Joshua's eyes on her. She glanced up from her notes app on her phone and caught him as he quickly turned away. She tried not to smile as she went back to her notes.

"A little background…your grandfather had his will drawn up about ten years ago. He even taped a message to you boys." Alex nodded at the family. "But, he had me in last Friday to change a small portion of it. I was planning to come in the following Monday with the changes for him to sign, but then…" He trailed off as everyone acknowledged Pappy's passing.

"Anyway," Alex continued, "that means that what was in the will ten years ago is what's legal and binding."

R.J. asked, "What portion did he want changed?"

"Well, he originally left the company to you, R.J.," Alex said.

Scout furrowed her brow as she caught Josh's surprised face out of the corner of her eye.

"We were in the process of updating it for…" Alex shrugged at R.J. "Well, a competition between the boys. Paps would have left it to whomever got the votes in the competition."

"What the hell?" R.J. glanced at the boys. When they didn't react, he asked, "Did you two know about this?"

"They weren't allowed to say anything," Alex said. "But now, with his death, it changes everything. Double Digits is yours R.J."

"Wait, that can't be legal," Lucas said.

"Alex, come on," Josh pleaded.

"I'm sorry, boys," Alex said. He looked apologetically at both of them. "There is something, though."

"What?" Josh asked.

"Tell us," Lucas said.

Alex caught R.J.'s attention before he spoke.

"R.J., you can run the company, you can sell it, or you can just appoint one son or the other. It's really up to you. It's your company now," Alex said matter of fact. "But you can also choose to continue the competition Pappy started."

"Dad," Lucas yelped. "Come on, let us compete."

Scout noticed Josh didn't say anything. He just considered his father's expression and then glanced to Alex.

"Didn't you say there was a video message?" Josh asked.

"Oh, right, yes," Alex said.

"Dad, before you make a decision, watch the video," Josh said. Everyone looked to R.J.

"I mean…" R.J. shrugged. "Fine."

While Alex pulled out his tablet and fiddled with it, Scout glanced at Joshua. He rubbed his temples and sighed. Her lips twitched with sympathy. It couldn't be easy for him or Lucas to lose their grandfather and then lose the company in the same week. *I hope R.J. does the right thing.*

"Okay, here we go," Alex said.

Paps popped up on the tablet screen. He sat behind his desk, the black and white photo of him and Bessie front and center.

"Well boys, I'm gone. But I'm happy. I'm dancing with your mother in heaven, R.J. You know the song."

"It's just the thought of you," R.J. whispered.

Paps sang lightly, "It's just the thought of you, and I forget to do…," he trailed off with a smile. "I'll give her your love son."

R.J. blinked back tears. As he did, Scout could feel her own tears gnaw at the backs of her eyes.

Pappy said, "I know we've had our differences. I know I pushed you too hard sometimes, but…I just wanted you to be a better man than I was. Dirty. Beaten. Broken. Until I met your mother. This company, it was a tribute to everything that made her special. It's yours now. Think of your mother and run it in her honor."

R.J. walked to the back of the room.

Pappy continued, "I know you believe she died because of her weight. And I've tried to tell you it wasn't…ah, hell," he sighed. "I love you son. No matter our differences, you made me proud every day I was alive. The most proud you ever made me was becoming a father. And being a damn sight better at it than I ever was. Thank you for that."

Scout could see that all three men were fighting back tears. She grabbed a tissue from her purse as she joined in.

"All of that leads me to my favorite grandsons. Oh, I just love ya both. We've all been buddies since you boys could walk. Remember those wasps, Josh?"

Scout peered at Josh and found he was already gazing at her. They both smiled as Paps laughed in the video.

"Lucas, remember that four-wheeler you crashed into the neighbor's Pitbull cage?

You're damn lucky that dog wasn't in there."

"Boy, was I ever," Lucas laughed.

"Lucky is right," Josh agreed.

"Josh, to you I leave the pond house. I know it reminds you of your mother. Go paint something beautiful there. And share the damn place with your brother."

Warmth and pain crossed Josh's face at the mention of his mother. *Paint something? Josh is an artist?*

"And to you, Lucas," Paps said. "I leave my Mustang. You know the one. Let your brother drive it now and again."

"Oh, hell no," Lucas said. He shook his head at Josh. Josh exhaled a bit of humorous air.

"Alex has the details on the rest of the stuff, like the money and all that. Have fun, boys. Live your lives. Find a good partner to settle down with. I love all three of you. More than you know."

Pappy faded out and Alex shut the tablet.

Everyone turned and stared at R.J.

"I need time to think," he said. Pain crossed his face.

"Understandable," Alex said. "I was working with Paps on the competition. All the sessions are set up and ready to go, starting tomorrow. If you choose to do the competition, and let one of the boys take over, we can start right away and just finish what Paps started."

"I'll have an answer for you later today, Alex, okay?" R.J. waved his hand into a stop motion. He was done talking.

"Okay," Alex said.

It was quiet for a moment before Scout finally asked the question that had been bugging her since she got Alex's text earlier.

"I'm sorry to interrupt right now but…"
Scout said quietly. Everyone turned to her.
"Why am I here?"

"Right," Alex said. "You're part of the
competition."

"I'm what?" she asked confused.

"I'll take you out to coffee and explain
everything, if that's okay?"

"Sure, I guess," she said.

"May I give your number to everyone,"
Alex asked as he waved at everyone in the
room. She nodded her approval. "Thank
you."

All three men got a phone notification as
her number slid into their cells. Watching
Josh enter her name into his phone was
particularly intoxicating.

Alex cleared his throat and sat his phone
down. "Initially, Paps wanted to have you
document the meetings and keep track of the

votes," Alex said. "But there was one other thing."

"What was that?"

"You were intended to be the tiebreaker."

"I'm sorry, the what?" she asked.

As it started to sink in, Scout glanced over to Josh as distrust planted a seed in her gut. *That's why he was suddenly interested in me.*

As Alex kept talking Scout locked eyes with Josh. Moments earlier, she would have pulsed heat through her stare, but now, it was ice. He looked caught. Or was that apologetic? Either way, she couldn't believe she fell for his charm.

Well, I won't let that happen again.

She scrolled through the notes she'd been making and typed in one last line: Call StudioX and set up the interview.

10

Buy Me Time

Josh saw the shift in Scout's eyes from trust to distance once Alex told her about her role in the competition Paps had set up. Now it looked as if he'd flirted with her only because he wanted her vote.

Wait…what do I want with Scout?

He quickly saved her number into his phone. A move that made his heart flutter a little as he typed out "Scout."

He waited until Alex had set up where to meet Scout later to discuss the competition and she excused herself to try and get her attention. She wasn't having it as she grabbed her things and walked out like the maven she was, with him in tow.

"Scout, wait, please," he said.

"I need to get ready to help with this competition if R.J. agrees, so we can talk later," she said coldly. She hit the button on the public elevator and waited patiently as he stepped up beside her.

"Scout, listen, I…" he started.

"You what?" she said. He saw an icy disinterest in her eyes. She was now a consummate professional and any inkling that she had found him even remotely interesting was gone.

"I…" he started. Yeah, what did he have to say anyway? Even though she'd been here for a few months, *he* had only just met her. They hadn't dated. They hadn't done anything. True, they had chemistry. But what had really transpired that he owed her any sort of explanation? *Nothing.*

Plus, he'd promised Lucas. So… "I guess…nothing."

"Right," she said. "Absolutely nothing."

He held her indifferent gaze and realized it was not nothing. Not to him, anyway. He did, indeed, feel *something* for Scout. What, exactly, he didn't know. But now he'd gone and messed it up before it even had a chance to get started.

"Scout, I…"

"I'll see you tomorrow, Josh," she snapped. "Good luck in the competition."

She stepped into the elevator and turned around, hitting the lobby button. She gave him one last glance and this time, there was something else besides a chilly disregard in her eyes. This time, there was a touch of hurt.

"Scout…" he said quickly and shot out his hand to catch the door, but it was too late. The elevator was gone, and so was she.

Now what? He was starting to feel very torn.

In more ways than one.

R.J. stared Alex down. "How long did you know about this?"

"You know I can't answer that, R.J.," Alex said. "Paps was my client. Not you. The competition was what he really wanted. Legally, it can't be enforced, but if you want to honor Paps and his final wishes, you'd let the boys fight for the company."

"To what end?" R.J. asked. "What was Pappy's intent here, Alex? That man never did anything without a plan. Whatever this little game is, it's not just about the company."

Alex sighed. "Paps had his ways. I don't know, exactly, what his point was, but, as you said… he always had a plan. I have a couple guesses, but…my job is to enforce the will. To help Paps get in death what he wanted."

R.J. blew a tight breath through pursed lips. *Alex is just doing his job.* R.J. nodded at him.

"He didn't legally change the will, R.J., but the boys doing this competition is what he wanted," Alex continued. "You can choose to honor it or not."

R.J. shook his head as he chuckled.

"God, that man was frustrating," R.J. huffed.

"Definitely could be," Alex said. "He also loved you. And those boys. Very much. I know that."

R.J. took in a deep breath and exhaled slowly. "I don't want his company, Alex."

"I assumed as much," Alex said.

"But I also can't say I want my boys to have it, either," he continued. "You know, my mom died because she was overweight.

So, this company, these clothes…you know,
I don't want to encourage it."

"I don't think that's entirely true," said
Alex. "Not according to what—"

"I know what Paps said," R.J. interrupted.
"And I don't care. It's why she died. Having
said that…"

R.J. glanced to the black and white photo
of Paps and Bessie.

"Let the competition go on. Let the boys
go through with it," R.J. said. "But, Alex, I
still want to proceed as though I'm selling it.
Can you privately put out feelers?"

Alex nodded begrudgingly.

"Good," R.J. said. "I need time to think.
And this will buy me time."

"Okay," Alex said cautiously.

"The first meeting is tomorrow?"

Alex nodded.

"What's the girl's name?"

"Heather," Alex replied.

R.J. acknowledged him, then turned to walk out. Alex stopped him.

"R.J., I know it's not my business," he started.

"Then stay out of it, Alex," R.J. nipped.

"I promise, I won't say it again. But…Paps, he showed me Bessie's medical records. They're in his safe. Your mom—"

"Like I said, Alex," R.J. interrupted. "Stay out of it."

11

High Energy

Scout walked into the shopping center Zumba class and immediately smiled at the instructor. She was a pretty blonde with a large build and a ton of energy.

"Let's go class!" The girl bounced as though her hot pink athletic shoes were spring-loaded.

Scout checked her notes. The woman's name was Heather, age twenty-five. The alleged stereotype was that plus-sized women were lazy and unmotivated.

"Not this girl," Scout said under her breath. What a stupid stereotype.

Scout could see that Heather was clearly athletic even though the blue-eyed wonder was maybe thirty pounds overweight or so. *She's a firecracker.*

Heather shouted, "Almost to the end! You can do this, people!"

She danced around as the Zumba participants excitedly kept up, drawing from her energy.

Scout scanned the workout room and spotted Josh in the mirrors toward the back, on the other side. A smile started to touch her lips, but she held back. *No. That wasn't real. Stay focused on your career.*

She sighed as she noticed R.J. and Lucas standing with him. R.J. had a dumbfounded look on his face as he watched Heather. Lucas, to his credit, danced in time with the instructor, encouraging her high energy.

He shouted, "Yes, girl, love it."

The instructor yelled back, "Thank you!"

Scout giggled at Lucas's contagious joy. The guy was a character, for sure Then, as if being lured by a siren at sea, her eyes found Josh's. He'd cast his gaze on her and was trying to catch and keep her stare, but she turned back to Heather. *Not falling for that again.*

As the music stopped, the instructor yelled, "Alright, class, great workout! See you all on Friday!"

Heather gave them a congratulatory air-punch then pumped her way back to Josh and Lucas. *That's my cue.*

Scout threaded her way through the sweaty bodies back to the boys. She was supposed to witness these interactions and keep track of the votes. And if she had to break the tie, she wanted to know what these women thought.

As she walked up, she overheard Heather say, "You must be Josh."

Her grip on his hand pulled him forward.

Surprised, Josh said, "Oh, hi, yes, yes I am."

She released him and Scout couldn't contain a tugging smile as he shook it off. Heather then turned to an enthusiastic Lucas.

Heather said, "And you're Lucas. My excited fan from the back of the room."

"That's me, girl. Come on in here."

He pulled her into a hug as she laughed with delight. Scout chuckled as Joshua rolled his eyes and R.J. raised an unimpressed eyebrow. *How can they all be so close and yet so different?*

After pulling out of Lucas's hug, Heather introduced herself at a quick clip. "My name is Heather and I just have to take a quick shower before we go is that okay with you guys?"

Josh hesitated. "Uh, yes?"

He looked questioningly at Scout, then Lucas.

Lucas said, "Absolutely, take your time."

Joshua couldn't keep up with how fast Heather spoke. On the flip side, Lucas kept right up with her. R.J. actively looked for a chance to introduce himself but there was no opportunity to do so. She was all business and spunk.

Heather said, "Great it'll just be a second then we can go I'm so excited about this restaurant I heard it was really good, did you hear the same thing?"

Josh shook his head. "Uh, I don't..."

Lucas recovered for him. "I totally heard the same thing! This restaurant *is* supposed to be amazing."

Heather said, "Great, I'll be out in just a sec."

"Uh…" Josh half-nodded.

"We'll be here," Lucas replied.

"Great." Heather turned and headed for the showers but stopped when she saw Scout.

"Are you Scout?" she asked.

"I am, yes. I'm the one that spoke with you, and the one you'll be in touch with after the meeting," Scout said.

"Oh, great! So nice to put a face to a name."

"Absolutely, the pleasure is all mine." Scout reached out her hand and Heather accepted. *Strong shake. I like it.*

"Are you eating with us, too?" Heather let go.

"Nope. R.J. and I…," she pointed to him, "…we'll be at the table next to you. So, you can have some quality time with both Josh and Lucas. Then later you and I will chat."

"Okay, perfect," Heather said. "I'll be right back then. Nice to meet you."

"You, too," Scout said. She glanced at Josh, who stood there for a second with a blank expression on his face before turning to look at Lucas, who smiled broadly.

"I'm winning," Lucas said. He held his hand up for a high-five from Josh, who ignored it. "Okay."

He put his hand down with a satisfied grin as R.J. shook his head in disbelief.

"Good grief, she's high energy," R.J. said.

"Blows that first stereotype out of the water, huh?" Scout said with satisfaction.

"She's definitely not lazy," Josh commented.

Lucas said, "Or unmotivated."

"Well, it's one girl, come on," R.J. said. He shrugged. "Doesn't mean anything."

Scout sighed. *He just will not let it go about fuller figured women.*

"Okay, well, just remember," she looked at Josh and Lucas. "You can't talk business at these things. The goal is to get to know her and let her get to know you so she can cast a vote for which one of you she thinks is best for Double Digits. Good?"

They both nodded.

Josh asked, "Besides the stereotype, why was she chosen?"

"Didn't you recognize the workout clothes?" Scout asked.

They both thought for a moment.

"Oh, yeah, that's last year's *Shine* line," Lucas said.

"Yep," she nodded. "And according to Alex, she's the company's number one customer. She spends thousands every year with us. So, she knows our brand. And loves it."

She glanced around to make sure most everyone had left the class, then turned back to the three men.

"She'll want someone running the business who can speak to her and what she needs from us."

Scout could see Josh was impressed with her and her research as he tried again to catch her eye. This time, she let him.

Josh said, "Knowing what she needs is important."

She couldn't help but lock eyes with him. Something about Josh spoke to her insides, warming them through and through.

Lucas gave Josh a punch to the arm, breaking the spell, as he said, "She's back."

R.J. and Scout quickly stepped to the side as Heather raced up and came to a screeching stop in front of the brothers.

She said, "Okay, I'm ready. Let's go!"

Josh flashed Scout a look of panic as Heather half-dragged him and Lucas out of the building. Scout couldn't help the small chuckle that escaped her lips as R.J. rolled his eyes.

Josh, Lucas, and Heather sat at a cozy table with white linen as Heather dominated the conversation.

"That was why I loved Double Digits because I finally had something beautiful to wear," she droned on.

R.J. rolled his eyes again. It was a move he was mastering during this absolutely ridiculous process. *Damn Paps and his stupid games.*

He and Scout had a front row seat to the nonsense at a table nearby. He was glad for that. He wanted to know what his boys were thinking and saying. Which is probably why Paps was going to cut him out of this thing all together. *Curmudgeon.*

He noticed Josh kept peeking at Scout and R.J. followed his gaze. *Huh.*

Scout was a beautiful girl, no doubt, but she was thick. *Too thick for my boy.* She was fine for him to work with, hell, maybe even have some fun with. But that's where it needed to end.

He glanced back to the table where Heather was once again going on and on, "Anyway, it was just—"

"Heather," Josh interrupted.

"What?"

Heather and Lucas looked at him.

"Just out of curiosity, do you ever slow down?" Josh asked earnestly. "You just, you know, seem super high energy. Doesn't that get exhausting?"

R.J. Smirked. He would have asked the same thing. *Good grief, who would need an upper with her around?*

"No, I don't think I ever have," she replied honestly. "I think my Mom tried to slow me down once, but…"

"Unsuccessful?" Josh asked.

"Clearly," she said. She shrugged.

Lucas said, "You know what, why slow down? I say, keep it going, girl. Look at you. Don't hide that."

Heather and Lucas laughed together as the waiter served them their dinner. Lucas looked at Josh like he was clearly winning.

R.J. smirked. Lucas was his wild child and the one he thought for sure would want to run *his* business, not Double Digits.

Secretly, R.J. wanted Josh to take it over. Josh was the oldest and the most sensible, which made him perfect for the job. But Paps never saw it that way.

Paps always thought Josh was a square peg forced into a round hole and that *Lucas* was the one better suited for running the companies. And R.J. had to admit that Lucas did seem to have his finger on the pulse of these women.

R.J. eyed Josh, who tossed a glance at Scout. R.J. quickly peered at Scout again as Scout smiled back at Joshua, then glanced back down at her plate. *What the hell?*

R.J. asked, "So, what do you think of all this?"

She turned to him surprised. *I guess I haven't really spoken to her all night, have I?*

"Well," she started, choosing her words carefully, "I think Paps was right to make sure both of them understood the women behind the company. But—"

"Yeah?" he interrupted.

The waitress put down their plates. R.J. eyed the steak and baked potato on her plate, as well as the butter pats and sour cream on the side. He peered at his plate with superiority. Its all-vegetable medley was a thing of beauty.

Scout continued, "I don't know he needed
to pit them against each other."

As Scout looked longingly at Josh, R.J.
took the opportunity to sneak the little cups
of butter pats and sour cream off her plate
and put them on a passing waiter's tray.
You're welcome, Josh.

"I don't know, those boys have been
competitive since birth," he said. Scout
flicked her green eyes at him. "Seems like a
natural way to do it for our family."

Scout shrugged. "Does Josh really want
to run the company?"

As Scout turned back to watch the boys
interact, R.J. took her baked potato and put
it in a flowerpot behind them, then moved
his steamed carrots to her plate.

R.J. said, "He loved his grandma more
than anything, especially after his mom died.
I think that's why he wants it so bad."

Scout turned back to R.J. "I'm sorry about that. I hadn't realized."

He tried to brush off her sincerity but the genuine warmth in her eyes made him pause. "Oh…thank you."

Scout glanced to her plate and spied the carrots with confusion. She glanced around the table, bewildered.

R.J. said quickly, "Your plate looks delicious. Let's eat."

He smiled as she gave him a suspicious look.

Scout sighed and started to eat, glancing at R.J. with a raised eyebrow.

Anxious to change the subject, he picked a topic he knew she'd like.

"Josh would hang around his grandma all the time. Especially just after his mom died. He was about nine years old," R.J. said. He had Scout's full attention. "At that point in her life, she was still modeling and trying on clothes for the company. And she was in her fifties, maybe sixties, I think."

R.J. paused for a moment remembering his mother. *She was a ballsy woman, for sure.*

"That was the last year she did it. She died a few years later," R.J. said quietly. He glanced at Scout, then started to pick at his food. He cleared his throat. "Anyway, I think Josh had good feelings from those experiences with her. And he's translated that to a desire to run the company."

"Interesting," Scout said. "So, they lost a mom and a grandma within five years."

"Yeah." R.J. moved his peas from one side of the plate to the other.

"And you lost a wife and a mother at the same time," she said pointedly.

He stabbed a pea from his plate then put down his fork. It clinked against the plate as he picked up his water and took a sip.

"That must have been terribly difficult," she said quietly. "And then to raise two sons by yourself. I can't imagine how trying that was for you."

He wanted to say something. He really did. But nothing would come out of his throat as he sat his water back down. He waited until Scout went back to eating to look her over. She was disarming.

He peered over at his boys and saw Josh glance again at Scout. When Josh saw R.J. staring, he turned quickly back to Heather. R.J. glanced at his dinner companion again.

Josh was like his mother. They were good at seeing people for what they were. So, if Josh saw something in Scout, then there was probably something beautiful there.

A text lit his phone as he glanced down. *From Alex: I've got two interested buyers. Still want to go down this path?*

R.J. glanced at Scout and then the boys before texting Alex back.

To Alex: Start the process.

He glanced at Scout. "You know, Scout," he began as she looked at him in surprise, "that's your name, right?"

"It is," she said. "I just wasn't sure you knew it."

I deserved that.

"I do," he said. "Anyway, I don't get why my boys want Double Digits and not my company. Why do you think that is? I mean, my audience and my company—they're not that different from Pappy's audience and company. All women want to look beautiful."

Scout put her fork down and took a moment to think through his question. It's a quality he had noticed in her and appreciated. *She's thoughtful about the words that come out of her mouth.*

"Well, it's a little more nuanced than
that," she said prudently. "Yes, women want
to feel like they're beautiful. But, really, it's
about women wanting to be the best version
of themselves that's possible."

"How's that different?" He started eating
again.

"Well, before Pappy's company and
companies like his, women who weren't
rail-thin or petite and small or models, didn't
really have clothing options that made them
feel their best, let alone beautiful. Clothes
and clothes shopping just made them feel
their absolute worst."

He put his fork down with gusto as it
clinked loudly.

"Well, maybe they shouldn't have
options," he said with determination.
"Maybe not having clothes that fit them is
what motivates them to get thin and
healthy."

She looked perplexed by his statement. "That's been consistently proven not to work and in fact has the exact opposite of the desired effect," she countered. "And thin isn't everything. Being thin isn't even indicative of good health in the same way that being overweight isn't indicative of bad health. It's all quite relative."

"We can agree to disagree on that one," R.J. said. He took a sip of his water and clanged the glass down.

"You asked me what I thought."

"Yeah, well," R.J. toyed with his food. "I didn't know you'd have such decent arguments."

He glanced at her as a smile bloomed at the corners of her mouth.

"I don't know why your sons don't want your company, R.J.," she said. "Have you asked them?"

He shrugged. "I've tried. Lucas…it's so simple with him. He wants to go where the money is. I get that."

He gave Scout a weary smile. "I make good money, but, not like Paps did."

"And Joshua?" she asked.

R.J. could see a light in her eyes when she said Josh's name even though she tried not to let on how interested she was in his answer.

"I can't quite put my finger on Joshua," he said quietly. "It's been like that since…"

He glanced at Joshua. *Since his mother died.* Since that day, he'd been a different child. One R.J. didn't feel like he knew.

He shrugged. "I guess I just don't know my sons as well as I thought I did."

He glanced up into a pool of warmth coming from Scout's eyes. *I can see why Paps trusted her. Why Josh wants to know her.*

"Geez, I never talk like this," he said. He rearranged his plate, his fork, his water glass, before settling his hands in his lap. "I apologize."

"It's okay," she said. "I don't mind."

Scout sighed as she tucked a long, dark hair behind her ear and cast her attentive eyes at Josh as the three polished off their dessert.

Heather said, "Alright, well, I guess it's time for me to vote. Plus, my boyfriend is waiting on me at the bar across the street. Drinks and dancing."

"That sounds like a blast," Lucas said.

She giggled with delight. "It really is."

Josh just smiled. *Josh just seems sad. Why? Paps?*

R.J. peered at Scout once more and this time he noticed how beautifully dressed she was, how carefully she attended to the details.

"Hmm," he murmured.

There were her expensive, but small, diamond earrings; the delicate gold watch; the carefully tailored navy-blue dress that embraced her curves; polished nails; and pouty lips.

And, of course, there was her heart and her mind. She was both warm and intelligent. She seemed liberated by any desire to please, while consumed by every desire to tell the truth.

Josh's mother was like that.

"It's been really great getting to know you both." Heather's voice cut through his thoughts like a sharp knife.

The waiter brought the check as Josh signed the bill. R.J. did the same.

"Thank you for dinner," Heather said.

"Of course. Thank you for taking the time to do this," Josh said. "It meant a lot to Paps. And it means a great deal to us."

"Absolutely," Lucas chimed in. "Great getting to know you, Heather."

"You, too," she grinned. She stood and they stood with her.

"Have a good evening," Josh said. He shook her hand.

"Girl, go have a great night with your man," Lucas said. He pulled her into a hug that delighted her.

"Oh, I will." She laughed as she shook her hips. Lucas mirrored her moves and she left the restaurant with a skip in her step. "Bye!"

Josh and Lucas turned to R.J. and Scout. Lucas bounded over to their table while Josh moseyed up behind him.

"How'd we do?" Josh asked. His eyes stuck to Scout.

"Great," she answered. "You followed the rules. And she seemed like she had a chance to get to know you both. So…now we wait."

R.J. asked, "So, how long will it take?"

Scout checked off date one on her phone, then glanced up at him. "I'm not...oh."

She peered at her phone.

"What?" they all asked in unison.

"I guess we didn't have to wait long," she said. She glanced between the boys.

"Who'd she vote for?" R.J. asked.

Scout flitted her eyes between Josh and Lucas as they stared questioningly at her.

"Well?" Josh asked.

"She voted for Lucas."

12

Am I Wearing a Sign?

"Josh, wait!"

Josh could hear Scout's voice, but he couldn't stop his legs from quickly carrying him to his getaway car. *I gotta get outta here.*

He wasn't quite sure if he was escaping the fact he had lost his first vote or if he was escaping the fact that after losing that vote all he wanted to do was sweep Scout into his arms and let her comfort him.

He shook his shoulders in a failed attempt to kick those complicated emotions out of his body and instead replaced his desires with something more potent.

"Damn it," he yelled. He banged his unlock button with his thumb at least ten times in a row unsuccessfully, yanking on the locked car door that refused to open.

"Josh, please," she said.

She was right behind him now and he could feel how close she was to his body. Every cell in his skin vibrated in her presence.

This was her fault. She was distracting him.

He whipped around on her. "What, Scout? What? I lost."

"You lost *one* vote, Josh," she corrected. She was calm and collected as she captured his gaze. "There are six more. It doesn't mean you've lost the company if that's what you want."

"What does that mean?" His voice swept up an octave higher than he meant.

"What?" She looked perplexed.

"*If* I want it…what does that mean?" He knew he was being too defensive. It was too much, and he could feel he was losing

control, but with no power to stop it.
Everything feels out of control.

"Am I wearing a sign that says I don't want this company or something?" he barked. "I want it."

That last bit he shouted. He was trying to convince her that he did want it. And she needed to know that. Everyone needed to know that. *He* needed to know that.

"Josh, I—"

"Stop, Scout," he said flatly. "You don't know me. We just met."

He straightened his tie and smoothed his suit as though Paps was standing right next to him. He did it one more time and felt himself recover. Back to the Josh he knew. That everyone knew.

"I didn't say I knew you," she said. She quietly backed away and he knew he'd hurt her feelings. *I didn't mean that.*

"I just...I just...," she stammered. She tucked a long, dark hair behind her delicate ear. He noticed it was adorned with a simple diamond and he suddenly wanted to kiss the spot right below it.

"I just wanted to reassure you that you had more opportunities," she said. "That's all."

Now that he was calmer, he could see he'd gone and done it again. Hurt her. Pushed her away. Which was the exact opposite of what he really wanted. *Wait, is it? What the hell do I want?*

"Scout, I'm sorry," he said quickly.

"It's okay," she said. She put another foot of distance between them. "I shouldn't have said anything. This is between you and your brother."

She took another step back and he lurched forward trying to close the gap between them. "Yes, but—"

"Josh, it's okay," she interrupted coolly. "Good luck in the morning at Kareena's house. The second meeting. I'll see you both there."

With that, she turned on her heel, walked to her small, white SUV, got in, and drove away.

Excellent. Way to push her away. Again.

Scout looked in her rearview mirror as Josh watched her drive off and she felt a pang of…*something.*

What is happening to me?

Normally, after an exchange like that, she'd write the guy off. Move on. Find someone else. The problem was, she had talked to Josh's father. And she had spent a lot of time with Paps. And both men talked a lot about Josh and Lucas. So, she knew Josh better than she should. Better than he realized.

And then she met him. *Oh boy.*

The chemistry between them had been electrifying. Running after him tonight when she'd seen the look on his face after Heather voted for Lucas felt like running after a boyfriend.

She had wanted to pull him close and comfort him, tell him it would be okay, tell him this might be a gift, an opportunity, to consider something else besides just running the family business. Or she could tell him he still had time to kick ass if that's what he wanted. Either way, those sentiments, those desires…they were the stuff of relationships. *And we're not in a relationship.*

But she was starting to wish they were. And that was evidenced by how close she had stepped to him tonight, closer than she should have, closer than was necessary. Within that inch or so that had existed between them her body had warmed to his. She'd wanted nothing more than to reach out and touch him, but she held back.

Lucky I did.

It was just another reminder that she needed to focus on her, not Josh.

Tomorrow, after Kareena's meeting, was her interview with StudioX. And even though her heart wanted to yank her attention to Josh and figure out what those feelings were between them, her mind was pulling rank and wrenching her back to reality.

After all, Josh was focused on *his* career, as evidenced by his reaction tonight. And that was okay. Appropriate, even. So, why shouldn't she feel the same for herself?

StudioX was proposing an opportunity she couldn't ignore. She needed to pay it its due. And that's exactly what she was going to do.

Josh or no Josh.

13

You Could Eat Off This Floor

Josh fidgeted with his tie as Lucas rang the doorbell of the cool, modern condo in the rich-looking neighborhood that Kareena lived in.

"Dude," Lucas said. He reached over and straightened Josh's tie for him. Josh smacked his hand away and loosened the tie.

Lucas widened his eyes in response. "Paps would roll over in his grave."

"Well, Paps isn't here, is he?"

Lucas gasped. "What the f—"

"Hey," Scout interrupted.

Scout and R.J. joined them on the small front porch that held a beautiful swing and a small, ornate outdoor table.

Damn it. Scout looked beautiful in an expensive knee-length, blue-gray sheath dress that fit her curves perfectly. His eyes trailed passed her hemline down her sculpted calves to her two-inch silver, strappy Jimmy Choo's.

"Josh?" R.J. asked.

"What?" He snapped his attention back up to their curious faces.

"Nevermind," R.J. said.

Josh saw a light blush cross Scout's cheeks as her eyes followed his suit line up to his messy tie. Her forehead crinkled at the lopsided silk before she landed on his stare.

I'm sorry. He didn't say it out loud, but he needed to. He wanted to. As if she heard him, she gave him an uncertain smile.

He felt that smile deep in his body, bringing many things to life as he returned her warmth. He started to apologize, but Kareena opened the door.

"Hi," she said. Already he could see that Kareena was a bright and bold woman.

Based on what Scout had told them this morning, Kareena was twenty-nine, a nurse practitioner, and she was breaking the stereotype that plus-sized women were dirty and unkempt. It was a bullshit generalization, and yet it had been a mantra he'd heard his father say a million times.

This girl was not that. Kareena was a breathtaking Indian vision with rich, dark skin and luscious lips coated in velvety cherry red.

"Well, hello," Lucas said seductively.

Josh hid a smile at her reaction, which was unimpressed by Lucas and his flirtations.

"Hi," she said coolly. She shook his outstretched hand. "I'm Kareena."

"I'm Lucas," he said, pulling back a little.

"I'm Josh." He stepped forward and shook her delicate hand. He was surprised at the strength of the handshake he received back. *Nice.*

"Good to meet you both," she said. She stepped to the side to allow them through the door. "Please, come in."

Josh guessed she was dressed in…*is that Calvin Klein? Those are definitely Blahnik's on her feet.*

"I'm almost ready for our meeting," she said gently. "I just need to call in an order for a patient. Please sit down."

She waved at her cream-colored luxury furniture that appeared as comfortable as it was lavish. She looked at her other guests. "You must be Scout and…R.J.?"

"We are," Scout said. "It's lovely to meet you. Thank you for your time and participation in this."

"Not a problem," she said. "As a new board member of the nonprofit arm of the company, I'm definitely interested in who will take over and what direction we're headed in."

She made direct eye contact with Josh and then Lucas, which Josh appreciated. She would be a real asset to their nonprofit, which did a lot of work for women and children in various areas. Josh had spent two years there before moving to the company under Paps. *I loved it there.*

"We need the right person running the company," Kareena continued. "So, I'm interested to get to know each of you beyond the business aspect. Who you are as people and how well you know the customer. Of which, I am one."

"Well, we're interested to know you, too, Kareena, so thank you," Josh said.

"Of course," she said warmly. "And I'm sorry for your loss. I had only just met Paps, but I could tell he really believed in this company and what it was accomplishing for women."

"It was for our grandmother," Josh said quickly. "She was really something."

Kareena smiled at him. "I'm sure she was."

Kareena's phone dinged. She typed something into it then politely excused herself. "I'll be right back."

"Take your time," Lucas chimed in, but she ignored him.

"This place is immaculate," Scout said. She started to wander around a little bit before settling into the cushions of the large bay window and letting the sunlight warm her face. *That would be a stunning photo.*

"And beautiful," Josh said. A heated glance passed between them before she pushed it away and looked back out the window.

He sighed and peered around him. Everything in Kareena's home was high-end and perfectly put together. Nothing was out of place.

"You could eat off this floor," Lucas said. He glanced at the hardwood floors and stylish rugs.

R.J. was noticeably quiet.

"Dad?" Josh asked.

"Yeah. Looks good." He shrugged as he tugged on his pant legs and sat down on one of the wingback chairs.

Josh knew his father. Knew when he was contemplating something. And he could tell, these women were throwing his previously held notions about full-figured women to the wind.

Whatever he'd tried to convince himself about plus-sized women, it was falling apart before his eyes.

As Lucas took a seat on the plush, oversized couch, Josh walked around her living room, glancing at all the photos. *A fulfilling life.*

There were photos with friends and family on vacations, parties, celebrations, all beautifully framed. One framed piece on her wall caught his eye as Kareena walked back in.

Kareena said, "Sweat and tears went into that."

He smiled as she walked up behind him to look at the framed medical degree on her wall.

"Harvard is impressive. You're an NP, right?"

"You got it," she said.

"Have you always wanted to be in medicine?"

"Always," she said. "I mean, my Dad is a doctor, so there was an expectation anyway, but I genuinely wanted to do it, too. To help people. Make a difference.”

Josh said, “That’s amazing.”

“You always want to run the company?” she asked him.

“Uh,” Josh paused as he contemplated the question. *Why am I pausing?*

“Are you specialized in anything?” Scout cut in quickly, saving him from making a fool of himself. He caught her glance with a quick nod of thanks as she returned a smile.

“Pediatrics,” Kareena answered. “I love kids.”

“I bet you’re really great with ‘em,” Lucas said.

“How can you tell that?” she asked.

“You just seem very warm. Friendly,” Lucas said, recovering nicely. “Kids pick up on that.”

Kareena said, “Ah. Well, thank you.”

She looked around at the group and said quickly, "Well, I hate to cut this short, but I do have patients. Shall we start?"

"Let's do it," said Lucas.

The conversation began as Josh got one final glance of Scout and melted on the inside from her smile.

Scout could barely contain the bright bursts of joy in her stomach when Josh had admired her. She had wanted him to notice her, wanted him to want her, and now she wanted more of it.

Wait. She shook her head for the third time since she'd arrived at Kareena's house remembering the last couple of interactions with him. *He's going through something. So, I need to stay focused.*

As they each said goodbye to the lovely nurse practitioner and walked out, she could feel Josh move to catch up with her. She slowed down a beat.

"Scout," he said breathlessly.

She got to her car and unlocked it, gripping the door handle but turning to face him.

"Hey, Josh," she said.

His cologne wafted her direction, and she inhaled the light notes of Sandalwood and musk. His face was cleanly shaven, and his dark hair was sculpted into gentle waves. His dark Armani suit was pressed and perfect, just like Paps would expect, but the tie was a crumpled mess. *What's happening there?*

"I need to apologize for being short with you last night," he said.

"Josh, you—"

"Please, Scout," he interrupted. "I'm sorry. I was frustrated and I took it out on you, and I apologize."

She could see the warmth in his eyes and knew he meant it. It made her legs feel weak.

"Oh, okay," she said softly. "Thank you."

"Also," he said as he glanced down and then back at her. "When you and I met…when you brought me my shirt…I didn't know about the competition. Or about you being the seventh vote."

"Oh," she said with surprise. If that was true, it would mean the chemistry between them that day was real. *Very real.* "So…"

"Yeah." He nodded and then smiled at her. A breath caught in her throat as a light heat started to make its way up her neck.

"Anyway," he continued, "I didn't mean to interrupt. I'm sure you have something you're doing, unless…unless you're free for lunch?"

"Uh." She paused. *Shit.* Her interview. "Josh, I'd like that, I really would, I just…"

I could reschedule my interview?

"I have something I need to do," she said. "Raincheck?"

She noticed the disappointment on his face and it hit her right in the gut.

"Sure," he said. "Absolutely, yes."

He stepped back as she slowly got in her car, as if the added time would change the outcome.

"But I'll see you this afternoon for the next meeting," she said. She settled in her seat and put her purse down. "Cali. We're meeting her at the Farmer's Market."

"Interesting," he said. "What's the stereotype on this one?"

"Um, let's see." She scrolled through her cell phone notes and read from them. "That

plus-sized women want to be that way——
all they eat is junk food."

She pulled her seatbelt on with
annoyance. "I feel very confident that R.J.
has put this one in your brain."

"He has." Josh tilted his head at her.
"What makes you so sure?"

"I'm pretty certain he took food off my
plate at the restaurant the other night." She
winked at him and half-laughed.

"He did what?" Josh questioned.

"Yeah. Pats of butter and sour cream
mysteriously disappeared off my plate." She
waved her hands in the air. "A baked potato
that looked oddly like mine was in a
flowerpot behind us."

"I'm sorry, Scout," Josh said. A flush
crossed his cheeks. "I'll say something to
him."

"No, absolutely not." She crossed her
hands in front of her. "It's not worth it. As

long as *you* don't think that. Though, with him as a dad, I can see where Paps would be concerned you might. Thus, this competition."

"Yeah, well," he mumbled. He loosened his tie again. "People change. I'd like to think I'm capable of moving beyond things I was raised on, you know?"

"I do," she said. She glanced at her watch. "I'm sorry, Josh, I need to get going."

"Okay," he said. He glanced down and back at her with a touch of disappointment. "I'll see you later."

"Yeah," she said with a smile.

As she shut her door and drove away, he gave her a little wave.

She was really torn now. The heat between them was real—it wasn't about the company. And she wanted to explore it. She wanted Josh. But she was almost certain she wanted this opportunity with StudioX, too.

As she pulled into the parking lot of a
coworking space where she rented a room
for her interview, she knew two things: First,
she wanted Josh *and* this amazing
opportunity. And second, she didn't want to
lie to him about it.

Which was exactly what she was doing
right now.

14

Pad Thai, Please

Scout's guilt was starting to nag at her as she glanced to Josh and Lucas standing opposite her and R.J. at the Farmer's Market as they waited for Cali. Her phone vibrated, so she pulled it out and checked it.

Text from Cali: Almost there!

Scout texted her back as she felt Josh's eyes on her. When she glanced up, he gave her a hopeful smile. He had been honest with her and now she felt she owed it to him to be honest about this job possibility. Her eyes flitted back to her phone.

Well, StudioX is likely not just a possibility—it's probably an offer.

Her interview had gone well. Very well. They loved her work, and there was a palpable good vibe among the group of them that had met. The CEO, the lead designer, the V.P. of Sales and Marketing…she'd met them all. Her role would be V.P. of Creative Services and she'd work hand-in-hand with everyone in the company to deliver the brand and its story to its customers, driving sales and opportunities.

I'd be great in this role. Plus, she'd already traveled numerous times to southern California and loved it. And now, to live there? *What an adventure.*

She peered at Josh. *He was a different kind of adventure.*

"Hi everyone," a bright voice rang out.

They turned to see Cali coming right toward them. She was thirty-one years old and lovely, which made her an excellent influencer for the Double Digits brand.

"Hi, I'm Scout, we spoke on the phone." Scout reached out her hand and Cali took it generously. "So nice to meet you."

"You, too," the size twelve social expert said as she smoothed down her leather pencil skirt and turned to introduce herself to R.J.

Cali had more than one-hundred thousand followers across social media. Her light eyes and wispy chocolate-brown hair that was loose around her plump face made her trustworthy and authentic. *Wow, she's got a great energy. Probably why Paps chose her.*

"Love your outfit," Lucas exclaimed. "That pencil skirt was our summer headliner two years ago. A bestseller."

"Oh, thank you," she said with a happy hitch in her voice, now turning to the brothers. She put her hands on her hips and posed like a supermodel for a second, her fitted baby blue button down cinched at the waist. "You know the quality of your clothes is unreal. I'll spend the money because I know it's going to last, you know? And the clothes are totes gorge."

"That's what we aim for," he said as he reached out his hand. "I'm Lucas."

She shook it with a smile. "Hi Lucas, so nice to meet you. Oh, and I'm so sorry for your loss."

"Thank you for that," he said. She shifted her stare to Josh.

"You, too. You must be Josh," she said. She shook Josh's hand.

"I am," he said. "So nice to meet you. And happy to hear and see how great our clothes are out in the real world."

"Thank you," she said. She glanced around at them. "Well, I know we have limited time, and I'm on a quick break, so I thought I'd shop. I need a few things for my dinner party tonight. Mind if I snap a few photos for my followers while I'm here?"

"Have at it," Josh said. "Can we help in any way?"

"Well," she said. "I'm on the lookout for some super ripe, very red heirloom tomatoes. If we can all keep an eye out for them, that'd be great."

Josh and Lucas nodded in synch. "Happy to help with that," Josh said.

"At your service," Lucas chimed in.

As the boys and Cali stepped out front and began shopping, R.J. and Scout fell back.

"How are you today?" Scout asked.

R.J. laughed. "Better. Again, my apologies for laying that on you."

"Not a problem," she said. "Paps used to do that, too. Talk to me. About random things. Sometimes, it's just easier to talk to a stranger."

"That's true," he said. He tucked his hands in his pockets.

"So, are these women surprising you yet?" She glanced at him as he raised an eyebrow at her. "I mean, Paps said in his video that the boys may have heard some of these stereotypes from you."

She shrugged gently and with a smile.

He laughed. "*May* have?"

He glanced guiltily at her. "My mom, she was sixty-eight when she died. Too young. Her weight…if she would have taken better care of herself…"

"I see," Scout said softly.

"I was thirty-eight. Anastasia, my wife, had just died two years earlier. Josh was ten. Lucas was eight. I just. I don't know."

"That must have been hard," Scout said quietly. "It was probably easier to blame her weight, be mad about that, have something to blame, instead of grieving such a terrible loss."

He halted and she turned to him. His face was flooded with a mix of complicated emotions, one of which was anger.

"I'm sorry," she said quickly. "I've overstepped."

There was an awkward silence that fell over them for a moment before he finally said, "Let's just get this over with."

"Okay," she said. As they started to walk, her phone went off. She glanced at her texts and a smile touched the corners of her lips.

"What?" he said gruffly. "What is it?"

"Kareena," Scout said. "She cast her vote for Josh."

Josh could tell he was winning with Cali. Unfortunately, so could Lucas.

"So, Cali," Lucas chirped. "What are you serving at your dinner party? Is it a celebration?"

"Not a celebration, no," she said. "I do a monthly dinner party for about twenty people. My followers love it. I show them how I shop, how I cook, how I dress, how I set the table…very Martha Stewart and Joanna Gaines type stuff."

"Sounds fun," Lucas said. "What's on the menu?"

"Tomato salad, beef tenderloin crostini, shrimp prima vera, and a berry dessert," she said.

"Sounds amazing," said Josh. "Do you eat like that all the time?"

"Always," she said. "I try to eat and cook clean, as much as I can. I love fresh fruits and vegetables. I rarely eat junk food. If I want a potato chip, I thinly slice sweet

potatoes and make them myself, you know?
Just better for you that way."

"Wow," said Lucas. "That's impressive.
Time consuming, though."

"Worth it," she said.

Lucas paused and stepped up to a wine
booth. "Do you have a wine yet?"

"I do," she said. "But do you have a
recommendation?"

As she stepped to the booth to talk wine
with Lucas, Josh glanced back to Scout and
found his father giving her a strange, angry
look.

"What the hell?" he whispered. His father
could be a bully sometimes, and Josh was
used to it. But he wasn't about to let his
father intimidate Scout.

He started to move toward them but
stopped when Scout glanced to her phone
and a smile touched her lips. He didn't know
what she said to R.J., but he knew what his

name looked like on her lips. *What's going on?*

As if summoning her gaze, she glanced to him with warmth in her eyes. She pointed at him and mouthed, "You got a vote."

He couldn't help the broad smile that lit his face. And for a second, he wasn't sure if that smile was because of the vote or because of the way she looked at him.

"Josh?" Cali asked.

"Oh, yes, sorry," Josh said. "Apologies. Did you find a wine?"

"I did," she said. "Lucas has good taste."

Lucas gave him a wicked smile as the two fell in step just behind her. When they did, Josh reached around and smacked the back of Lucas' head.

"He certainly does," Josh said, as he mouthed to Lucas, "Kareena voted for me."

Lucas punched him in the gut and as Josh doubled over, Lucas stole Cali's attention and asked her about tomatoes and Turner's Tea—a Pittsburgh staple.

Josh glanced back to Scout, who raised a humorous eyebrow at him. He straightened back up and winked at her before turning back to Cali and Lucas. *Did I just wink at her?*

He smiled to himself as he stole one more look at Scout. She was grinning.

I did wink at her. And she liked it. Me too.

He pulled out his phone. He had avoided texting Scout on purpose. He knew that once he opened that flood gate he wouldn't be able to close it. But now…now he felt ready. He exhaled a breath as he completely undid his tie and pulled it off his body. He shoved the tie in his pocket and unbuttoned the top of his shirt. He started to type.

Josh: I need to work on the next magazine at Paps' office tonight. Care to join me and help out? Dinner's on me.

He hit send and waited. Why did the seconds between sending a text and getting one back feel so damn long? His phone dinged.

Scout: I'd love to.
Josh: Chinese food?
Scout: Perfect. Pad Thai, please.
Josh: Excellent. Meet you there at 7.
Scout: Looking forward to it.
Josh: Me, too.

Josh felt lighter somehow as he rushed to catch up with Cali and Lucas. He wasn't even sure what they were talking about, but he didn't care. He was going to finally spend some quality time with Scout.

It was the most alive he'd felt in a very long time.

15

New Beginnings

Scout pushed the elevator button to the C-Suite of Double Digits and grinned from ear to ear.

When she had seen Josh's name pop up on her phone at the Farmer's Market, a tingling sensation had coursed through every cell in her body.

When she read the text he sent, parts of her body responded in ways she hadn't felt since her last relationship, but much, *much* stronger.

She wanted Josh. And her body was in tune with her heart.

As the elevator dinged on the top floor to let her out, she felt a rush of happiness, and then one of dread.

Should I tell him about the job offer?

She scrolled through her emails quickly and pulled up the one that said, "Official Job Offer" from StudioX.

If it had been Paps, she would have waited until she got this very offer to tell him she was leaving. He would have wanted her to stay, she knew that, but she'd have gone anyway. The offer was too good. The money was too much. The C-Suite track they wanted to put her on was everything she wanted.

But this isn't Paps. This is Josh. And I'm falling for him.

She put her phone away in her bejeweled pocket purse and stepped off the elevator. She had chosen a pair of dark, fitted jeans, a sleek white tank top and a soft leather jacket in a navy-blue color that made her eyes sparkle. Her hair was soft around her face with big beach curls and her burgundy lipstick made her pout particularly alluring.

As she stepped into Pappy's office, she had to catch her breath. Josh was already there taking the plastic food containers out of the bags and putting them on the coffee table in front of the leather couches.

She'd never seen him like this before. His hair looked like he'd simply run his fingers through it and walked out the door. It was loose and wavy on top with one long strand falling across his sparkling espresso eyes. His casual joggers fit loose around his taut hips and showed off his assets, while his expensive T-shirt fit snug against his muscled chest and arms.

Josh in a T-shirt and joggers? Swoon.

"Hi," she squeaked out.

He turned quickly and before he could speak, he stopped himself, taking in her face and figure. She could see the desire cross his face as he took a breath.

"Scout," he said lightly. "You look, uh…" He paused and let his eyes finish the sentence as she felt a jolt of electricity zap her gut.

"Thank you," she said softly. "You, too."

"Uh, dinner," he said as he recovered. "Best Pad Thai in the city."

"Yum," she said. She walked further into the office and set her purse on one end of the couch. She could feel his eyes on her as she removed her jacket, her fitted tank top doing its job.

"Where should I sit?"

"Wherever you like," he said. When she sat on the couch next to where he stood, he placed her food in front of her along with chopsticks and a fork. "Not sure which one you wanted."

"Chopsticks, of course, thank you," she said.

"Wine?" he asked.

"Sounds good."

He hurried to grab the glasses from Pappy's bar cart, then pulled a bottle of wine from the bag that held the food.

"I actually got it at the Farmer's Market," he said. "It looks great."

He poured her a glass of the rich, red vino, then one for himself before placing his food right next to hers. He sat down softly, picking up his glass and raising it.

"To…" he said, pausing.

"Paps and his amazing company," she finished. "And—"

"New beginnings," he interrupted. They each smiled as their glasses clinked.

"New beginnings," she whispered. She took a sip and felt the smooth Cabernet slip down the back of her throat. Almost immediately she could feel the warmth in her belly. *Or maybe that's Josh.*

"It's delicious," she said.

"It is," he agreed. "Shall we?"

He waved at the food.

"Yes," she said. She felt a bright smile bubble up from her gut as they took their chopsticks and dug in.

"Oh," she said with her mouth full. "This is amazing."

He laughed with his cheeks full of lo mein noodles. "So good."

Scout spied photos and layouts on the other side of the table and picked them up.

"These are looking great," she said as she chewed her food. "Like, really great."

"I like what you're doing with the simple layout and the way you're organizing the clothes," he said.

"Thank you," she said. She gave him a winner's grin as she took a sip of wine.

A little moment of mutual admiration shuffled between them.

"Okay, listen," he said. He took another bite, chewed, swallowed, and prepared to say something serious. "I don't get it."

"Get what?"

"What's the deal with women, beautiful women, trying so hard to be a size two, or whatever?" He waved his hand. "I don't understand. It's simple, isn't it? Don't women just want to have great clothes and look nice?"

He pointed to her.

"Look at you," he said. "You're beautiful. Period."

Scout gave him a "I call bullshit" look.

"Yeah, okay, I mean, I get it," he said. He acknowledged her callout as he took a drink of wine. "But I don't get it."

She finished her bite and took her own drink of wine before answering. She wanted to be as thoughtful as possible since it appeared he was being genuine in asking the question.

"Well, traditionally, to be blunt, the size twos of the world have rings on their fingers, and the other girls don't," she said. "And, over time, instead of men changing to accept women, women have been forced to become the size twos of the world, even when it's not possible."

"How do you mean not possible?" he asked.

"I mean, most models are five-foot, ten-inches and one hundred and twenty pounds, right? They're the girls at your dad's gym," she said. "And I support those women as much as any woman. But what does a girl who's five-foot, three-inches tall and one hundred and forty pounds do for the same attention?"

She shrugged and took another sip of wine. "The list of examples of how women don't stack up is ridiculously long. And for many of them, their physical appearance is out of their biological control."

She raised an eyebrow at him as he looked at her with a thoughtful stare. She was starting to really appreciate that part of his personality. The part of him that stopped and thought things through. He, maybe, wasn't as spontaneous or zealous as Lucas, but he had other, more graceful qualities, like this one.

"What?" she asked.

He smiled, got up, and walked across the office. He grabbed his phone, the black and white photo of Paps and Bessie, and walked back, sitting down next to her. He put the photo on the table and held his phone.

She scooted a little closer to him and in response, he scooted closer to her, sharing his screen. She tried to concentrate on what he was doing—scrolling through the Double

Digits website—but having his thigh against hers, his arm against her arm, his cologne filling her senses, was a distraction. *Kiss me.*

"So, they come to us," he said.

"Huh?" she said, trying to rouse herself out of his spell.

"You asked what the shorter girl, who's heavier, does when she wants to feel good and have the attention." He looked at her and tilted his phone to her. "They come to us. Right? Because we're not trying to make them something they're not. We're trying to make what's great about them come through."

He smiled at her, and she could tell he was hoping for her approval.

"Yeah," she said quietly. "Exactly."

Josh broke her gaze to put down his phone and pick up the black and white photo of Paps and Bessie. He held it between them so she could see it, too. It was a lovely photo.

"He loved her, no matter what," said Josh. "Did you know that when he married her, she was actually around a size ten. But she gained some weight when she got pregnant and after she had my Dad, she could never lose it."

"Very common for most women," she said.

"Right. And, according to Paps, back then, it wasn't always easy for women to find bigger clothing that was stylish. Or made them feel good."

"That's true even now," she smirked. "But, definitely worse then, when your grandma would have been dealing with it."

"Right," he said. "So, Paps, who owned a Lazarus...do you remember Lazarus?"

Scout laughed, "No, but I know of it from school."

"Me too," he laughed. "Well, Paps owned one. And when he couldn't order in any clothes that my Grams felt beautiful in, he found designers who would make them for her. One thing led to another and, pretty soon, Double Digits was born."

"*That* is the back story?" Scout asked. She always knew it was in honor of Bessie, but she didn't know all that. *Paps was such a good man.*

"Yep," Josh said proudly. "Paps didn't cheat. He didn't get mad. He didn't leave. He loved her so much, thought she was so beautiful, that he put in his money and his time to find a way to help *her* feel beautiful after pregnancy. This place was his love letter to her."

Scout dabbed at her eyes with her fingertips. "Oh geez, I'm sorry," she said as the tears started to prick at her eyes.

"Just…beautiful story. Paps was…something."

"He really was," said Josh. "Ahead of his time, really."

Josh put the photo down and turned to Scout.

"I see both sides, ya know?" he said. "I see Pappy's version of the world. And I see my dad's version of the world."

As she wiped her eyes dry, she asked, "And what's your version?"

"Somewhere in between, I suppose," he said. "I lost my mom and my grandma within a few years of each other. I would have blamed anything for that pain."

Without thinking, Scout reached out and lightly touched his face with her fingertips, pulling him to look at her.

"I'm sorry, Josh, that you went through that," she whispered. "I really am."

They locked eyes and she could feel her body lean into him without her even trying. He leaned in, too, and slowly made his way to her lips.

She could barely breathe as he first touched his lips to hers then let out a soft moan as her fingertips trailed from his face down his throat and to his chest.

"Josh," she moaned. His hands clutched her waist as his thumbs rubbed slow circles on her lower abdomen. It sent shockwaves through her pelvis down to her toes. The pressure his lips placed on her lips became more urgent and just as he parted them with the tip of his tongue, a familiar voice broke the magic.

"What's goin' on in here?" Lucas cackled.

Scout and Joshua quickly moved away from each other.

Josh snarked, "Your timing is impeccable, Lucas."

Lucas smiled broadly. "It really is, isn't it?"

Scout could feel Lucas's stare on her so she turned to face him.

"Heyyyy Scout," he taunted. He shoved his hands in his pockets and smiled. "How are you two lovebirds tonight?"

Such a little brother move.

"What do you want, Lucas?" Josh snapped.

Lucas shrugged. "Dad said you were here, so I came to see if you heard from Cali," he said. He looked Josh over with a quizzical stare. "Dude. You came out of the womb in a suit. What the hell are you wearing?"

"Lucas," Josh warned.

"Alright," he said. He walked to the coffee table and grabbed a handful of candy, shoving several pieces into his mouth as he plopped down. "Kareena's vote must have been a fluke, right? So, just want to make sure it gets back on track."

They both looked at Scout.

"Her vote wasn't a fluke," Scout said sharply. "Her take on it was that Josh had the warmth and professionalism to run the company."

"Sure, sure." Lucas shrugged. "She didn't see those joggers."

"Lucas, I swear to God," Josh seethed.

"What'd Heather say about me?" Lucas questioned.

Scout sighed. *I like Lucas, but geez, he can ruin a moment.*

"She noted that your energy and enthusiasm were vital for moving the company into the future," Scout said.

"And Cali?" Lucas asked.

"I haven't checked."

They each gave her a prodding stare.

"Gee, let me check for you," she said reluctantly. Under her breath, she added, "Not like I had a night going or anything."

She got her phone out of her purse and checked her messages. The one on top was from Cali. She popped it open and felt her stomach drop. *Shoot.*

"Well?" Lucas prodded.

"Lucas," she said quietly. She locked eyes with Josh, and he gave her a half-smile and nod. *Damn it.*

"She say why?" Josh asked.

"Ummm," Scout said. Cali had said why but she was hesitant to tell them. Mostly because she was part of the reason why. "Yeah, she said Lucas seemed tuned into the social media world and was high energy and that Josh seemed…"

"Yeah?" Lucas prodded.

"Distracted." She gave an apologetic shrug to Josh who just grinned at her.

"You don't say," Lucas said. He shot forward in his seat, his arrogance making him practically glow. "I wonder why."

A glance passed between the brothers. *I should probably go.*

"Thanks for dinner, Josh," she said. "I better head out."

She grabbed her purse and smiled at him.

"I'll walk you out," he said.

"No, I'm okay," she said. "There's a security guard in the lot. And I'll see you both tomorrow. We have the final three women all in one day. So, all of us probably need some rest."

"Night, Scout," Lucas said. She tried to give him a dirty look, but it was basically impossible. Lucas was annoying, but charming as all get out. Just like a little brother would be.

"Night, Lucas," she said with a smirk. She started to leave, then turned back, walked quickly to the coffee table, snatched the candy bowl, and left.

"Hey!" Lucas yelled.

She heard Josh laugh as Lucas said, "I like her."

Smiling to herself, she startled when she heard Josh right behind her at the elevator.

"Scout, wait," he said.

She turned to face him as he closed the space between them. "You can have the candy back."

She shoved the bowl playfully into his stomach as he chuckled and took it.

"I'm dumping this in the trash."

"I support that," she said. They shared a hot, steamy second as her body fired up in his presence. "I'm sorry I distracted you today."

She only half meant that, and he knew it.

"You have nothing to be sorry for."

She leaned in but he stopped her.

"Scout, I…" he paused.

"What?" she asked.

He sighed. "Lucas picked up on our chemistry a while ago," he said. "And, well, you're the seventh vote. Despite what was happening five minutes ago, I did make a promise to him. To…finish this process first. Before anything…"

"Oh," she said. *Of course.* Of course he promised Lucas he wouldn't get involved with her. She understood that. But, still…*great. Just great.* "I get it, yeah."

"But also," he said. "I'd like to actually take you on a real date. In a restaurant. You know, pick you up, drive you there. The whole nine. Not Chinese food in Pappy's office."

Her knees almost buckled under the weight of his seductive stare.

"I'd just…I'd just like to have this business stuff past us before we do that," he said. "Just…a clean slate."

"Clean slate, yeah," she said. She didn't love it, but she understood it. And she appreciated he wanted to do it right. A lot of men wouldn't. But, she was quickly learning, Josh was not like other men.

And speaking of clean slate.

"Josh, there's something I need to tell—"

"Josh," Lucas interrupted. "Dad just called. He wants to see us at the house."

"Okay," Josh said. "Hang on."

He turned back to Scout. "You were saying?"

"You know what, we can chat later," she said.

"You sure?" he asked.

"Yeah, I'm sure," she said.

He kissed her on the cheek, lingering there for a moment as they listened to each other breathe. "Goodnight, Scout."

"Goodnight, Josh."

He pulled back and stepped away as she turned and got on the elevator. He gave her a little wave.

When the doors closed, she let out her held breath. *Holy hell, I'm so into him.*

She opened her phone and re-read the job offer.

I'll tell him later about StudioX.

16

Fathers Know Best

R.J. stared at his computer screen then glanced at a photo of him with Paps, Josh, and Lucas.

"R.J.?" Alex asked.

R.J. turned back to the computer. "I heard you, Alex."

"I think you need to reconsider this," Alex said from his home office. "This is not what Paps would have wanted. At all. Selling the company? He's probably rolling over in his grave."

R.J. glanced at the photo again.

"Paps could never see what I see," R.J. said.

Alex responded, "And what's that? The cash? He wouldn't want this. And selling Double Digits out from under your sons won't lead them back to you and taking over your business."

"That's not…" R.J. trailed. He shook his head. "That's not why."

"Then why?" Alex pressed.

"Dad?" Lucas yelled from the front door of the pond house.

"I have to go, Alex," R.J. said.

"R.J.—"

"I have to go," R.J. interrupted. He shut off his computer.

Katherine walked down the hallway and leaned against the doorframe of his office.

"Is this the right thing?" R.J. asked nervously. "Alex is right. Paps would absolutely spit fire."

Katherine sighed and looked him over. "Sometimes fathers know best. And sometimes they don't," she said. "Talk to the boys, R.J. And when you're done talking, for once in your life, listen."

She gave him a half-hearted smile and walked toward the front of the house as she yelled, "Hi boys!"

R.J. glanced at the picture again before turning around to the other side of his desk and picking up a stack of papers. He looked closely at them again. "Autopsy report," it read. "Aortic Aneurysm." "Medical Anomaly." "Unrelated to risk factors."

R.J. glanced at the name of the patient. His mother. Bethany. Nickname, "Bessie." His eyes misted over as he took a deep breath. He reached to the glass of whiskey sitting next to the stack and took a swig. He dried his eyes and put on a fake smile as he walked out the door.

R.J. could see immediately when he walked in the living room that Josh knew something was up. The kid had never been blind to when R.J. was being fake.

"Dad?" Josh asked. *Yep. No niceties. He just wants the bottom line.*

"No hug?" R.J. asked.

Lucas glanced at his father and then Josh as Katherine sat down on the couch in the sunken living room.

"Okay, what?" Lucas asked. He nervously looked between R.J. and Josh. "What's happening right now?"

The three of them had a stare down worthy of a western movie. R.J. finally broke the silence.

"I have an offer for Double Digits," he said. "I think we should sell the company."

"You son-of-a-bitch," Josh spit.

Josh had never spoken to him like that. To anyone like that. It had never been his style.

R.J. was surprised, but also a little proud. *He's becoming his own man.*

"You must be joking?" Lucas spat. "Dad? Say it's a joke."

"I'm not kidding. And it's not a joke," R.J. said calmly.

"Selling Pappy's company won't make us come running to yours," Josh emphasized. R.J. could see the tension in Josh's face, the red blush sweeping up his neck. "That company was for grandma. For the love they shared. It's our family…crest. Honor. Whatever. It's what our whole family was built on."

"It was," R.J. said. He felt the tears hit his eyes. He quickly wiped them away and cleaned himself up. "Their love…stuff of movies, you know? It's the same way I loved your mother. And now Katherine."

He glanced at her, and she smiled with a nod of support.

"You support this?" Josh turned to her as though a snake had bitten him.

"Josh," she said quietly. "I think, maybe, just listen to what your father has to say. Just this once."

"Dad?" Lucas asked. "Explain yourself. This is my future, too, not just Josh's."

R.J. swallowed as he looked at his boys. *They're so angry with me.*

"Just let me talk for a second," he said. He put his hands out in a stopping motion. *They're gonna hate me. But I'll hate myself more if I don't at least say it.*

So, say it.

"Please," he said.

He could see that Lucas was more open to his words than Josh, who held so much venom in his eyes that R.J. could barely take it. But he knew, Katherine knew, he had to set it up this way.

I need to give Josh an out. He may not realize it. But he will.

Josh and Lucas both relented and he held the floor.

"Just to be clear, I haven't sold Double Digits. I just have the offer," he said. "It's an offer that could set you both up."

He saw Lucas's eyes light with curiosity. Josh just shook his head.

"Paps and I, we were lucky bastards. Paps found Bessie, fell in love, and out of that, we have our family," R.J. said. His hands were telling the story with him. "We have an amazing couple of businesses, we have a lot of things other people only wish for. We're so…not lucky, but, yeah, blessed. And I never use that word. But we are."

R.J. saw Josh shift his feet at that word. Josh wouldn't call losing his mother or his grandmother any of those things.

"I had Anastasia," R.J. said as tears choked his throat. He stopped to catch his breath and felt his sons' stares upon him. He had never cried in front of them. Not once. *Pride.*

When he looked up, they both had glistening eyes.

"Losing her almost killed me."

He felt the first tear slide down his face, and then another. He swatted at them and tried to compose himself but couldn't when he saw his sons struggle through their own grief, too. It took a second for all of them to regain their composure.

"And then I met Katherine, and I thought, how did I get so lucky to find love twice, huh?" R.J. smiled at the boys as he cleaned up his face. They responded in turn before then acknowledging Katherine.

"And that all made me start to think that, instead of telling you boys about love, instead of celebrating what we did have, I spent most of my time as your father being angry," he said. He gave them an apologetic nod.

"Maybe, on some level, I was teaching you to avoid loss," he said. He put his hands on his hips. "What I never said to either of you is…I'd suffer through any pain to have those precious moments with your mother. To have you kids."

He sniffed, then wiped his nose with his sleeve as Lucas swatted at the tears in his eyes and Josh wiped his nose.

"Paps used to tell me that about my mom. That, the loss is as great as the love," he said. "And if you want to avoid loss, by all means, avoid love. Avoid things that make you truly happy. Protect yourself from ever feeling the pain."

R.J. choked up again and saw in his sons that he had been right in what he did. The sorrow and the relief on their faces that they finally heard the truth from their father, told him that.

"I've prevented you from living your lives. From finding real love," he said. He looked right at Josh. *I know how he feels about Scout.* "I'm not going to do that anymore."

He recovered quickly and said the thing he felt finally needed to be said.

"I won't sell Double Digits and I'll honor Paps and his competition, *if...*" he paused and waited for their full attention, "*If* that's what you really want."

He looked right at Josh.

"But if it's not, if you don't love it the way you thought you did, if there's something, or someone, else that's better suited for you, I've set up your out for you," he said.

He waited until that sunk in.

"We can sell the company, and you can go live your lives how *you* want to live them," he said. "Without feeling obligated to Paps, or me, or the grief you've held onto for so long. Too long."

He looked at Lucas, who smiled back at him and nodded.

"Thank you for that," Lucas said quietly.

R.J. looked at Josh, who was struggling to keep his composure. It was unusual for Josh, who was the "always put together" son. But he could see now, in the two boys, that he had been wrong about that.

It was Lucas who had dealt with his grief and had become exactly who he was. It was Josh who had struggled and put on a mask. *That was my fault.*

"I'm sorry, Josh," he said quietly. Josh sunk his stare into R.J. "I relied on you too much, as the oldest, to get through it all. I pretty much assured you'd always have this ultra-tough exterior when what you really needed was your father to be your father, so you could just be my son."

He held Josh's painful stare for a moment.

"I'm giving you that now," R.J. choked out. "I'll support whatever you do next, as long as it's what *you* want."

No one said anything as the truth of the situation lie exposed and bare in their living room. R.J. didn't know if Josh would ever forgive him, but he hoped this was the olive branch that could bring him closer to his sons.

And maybe, finally, allow them to find happiness on their own terms.

17

Love or Money?

Scout carefully tucked her hair behind her ear as her long locks gave off a 1950s dramatic wave look. Her red lips were pert and pouty.

She may have to wait for this competition to be over to have a first date with Josh, but until then, she'd make him want her every day leading up to it. She glanced at her watch. *They're late.*

"Hmmm," she mumbled. She checked her phone. *Nothing.*

Finally, R.J., Lucas, and Josh walked slowly through the door. R.J. sat with her, while Josh and Lucas took a table beside them at the window. Josh's hair was barely combed, his tie was M.I.A., and his suit wasn't pressed. *Oh, my. What's going on?*

She glanced at R.J. "What's wrong?"

"Nothing," he said. He shook his head and smiled at her. "What's the stereotype on this woman? Uh, Honor?"

"Oh," Scout said at his sudden change of subject. "Uh, that plus-sized women are insecure and don't date as much or have as much sex."

"Now see, even *I* don't believe that stereotype," R.J. said. He pulled out his most charming grin. "Paps was wrong about me believing that one."

She was surprised at his sudden change in demeanor. Yesterday he was angry at her comment, today he was open and caring.

"Oh, yeah?" she asked tentatively. She glanced at Josh, who wouldn't look at her. "Josh seems really—"

"Josh will be fine," he said quietly, shutting her down again. "Let's get these final three meetings done. We'll go from there, okay?"

He was kind, but firm. *Do they know about my interview?* And now she was panicked. She had meant to tell Josh yesterday about it, but she wasn't ready. Mostly because she didn't know what to say. Or what she was going to do. But now, today, she was regretting that. *I should have told him.*

"Is this about me?" she asked.

"Why would you ask that?"

"I just…I meant to tell Josh about the offer—"

"How do you know about the offer?" he asked suddenly.

"What?" she asked confused. "Because it's my offer."

"Wait," he shook his head. "What offer are you talking about?"

"Well, what offer are *you* talking about?" she asked.

They stared at each other for a moment as a gust of air made them blink. They turned to the door to see it swing open and everyone in the coffee shop looked up to see twenty-five-year-old Honor.

"Wow," R.J. said impressed.

"Right?" Scout agreed. Honor was an African American beauty with gorgeous legs that stretched for miles and miles. Her face, wrapped in aviator sunglasses, put to shame every supermodel on every glossy magazine cover ever. Fashion bloggers idolized her as their daydream.

The silky goddess stopped her catwalk abruptly at Josh and Lucas's table.

"You, Josh?" she asked to Josh, who didn't notice her. She switched her stare to Lucas. "You Lucas?"

"Good God in heaven, yes, I'm Lucas," he said with a wide smile. He stood up and pulled out her chair for her. "And you are stunning."

"Thank you, gorgeous," she said.

As she sat down, Scout glanced at Josh, who just stared out the window. When Lucas sat down, he slapped Josh in the side, getting him to finally pay attention.

"Hello," Josh said half-heartedly.

She smiled as she removed her sunglasses, revealing beautiful violet eyes.

The waiter walked up as she glanced to him.

"Uh...co-coffee?" he stuttered. "I mean, do you want some? I mean, do you want coffee? Or, anything? I could get you anything you want. Anything at all. It's yours. Anything. Coffee?"

"Aw, you're sweet." She grinned at him. "I've been out all night and I need some caffeine. Give me the biggest, blackest, tallest cup o' java you got."

"Yes, ma'am," he said exuberantly. "I mean, you're not a ma'am. You're beautiful. I mean, not beautiful, I mean you are beautiful, just, I wasn't calling you beaut—"

"Just bring me the coffee," Honor interrupted.

"Okay," he said. He walked away and she turned her stunning gaze onto Lucas, then Josh.

She said, "I feel like I know both of you already."

"How's that?" Josh asked, finally joining the conversation.

"Well, I knew Paps. God rest his beautiful soul," she said. "He talked about you two all the time. Showed me pictures."

"Wait, what?" Lucas said surprised. "How did you know Paps?"

"I'm a designer," she said. "Paps picked up my line right before he passed. He said he was tryin' to freshen it up. He did it off the word of a girl named Scout. Found my line and brought me in."

Scout heard her name and when it came out of Honor's mouth, Josh turned to her. He tried to smile, but it seemed hard for him. The look in his eyes made her catch her breath. He looked pained, confused, but also…was that happy? *To see me. He's happy to see me. I don't understand.*

Josh turned back to Honor.

"You're the designer for Scout's Honor clothing line, exclusively for Double Digits," Josh said.

"You got it," she said with a smile.

"Your stuff is gorgeous." He drummed his fingers on the table. "I saw the line in the next issue. We were supposed to meet next week."

Lucas interrupted, "Wait…you're a plus-size designer? You are no way plus sized."

"I'm a size ten/twelve. That's plus sized in the fashion world," she said. "I'm downright disgusting."

She smiled big as her waiter delivered her coffee.

"And while we're at it, I don't use that negative word. Plus sized. Get rid of that," she said as she took a sip. "I make beautiful clothes for beautiful women, period. I don't even use numbers in my sizes. You're either a Queen, or a Princess, or a Rock Star, or a Vixen, but you're not a number."

"How does a woman know what to buy?" Josh asked.

"She knows," Honor said. "She can pull up a pair o' pants, hold it out and guess if it's close to her size. Pretty soon, she knows which one she is. And she'll always feel good about buying a size Rock Star. Same can't be said for buying a size sixteen or twenty-eight or twelve. I'm not about makin' women feel bad for wanting to be beautiful as they are."

"I can see why Paps wanted you and your clothes," Josh said.

"He was a beautiful man," she said. "You're both lucky you had him."

"We are," said Lucas.

"I know we're not allowed to talk shop today, but I will say that Paps has a beautiful thing going," she said. "It just needs a little makeover. That Scout girl, the consultant, he's been working with, she's got some good ideas. I dig her vibe."

"Yeah," Josh said. A smile played at the corners of his lips. "Me, too."

"She's done some great work," said Lucas. "Did you see the most recent magazine?"

"I did," she said. "It's gorgeous. It's why I agreed to be part of it. I'd be proud to have my clothes associated with your company."

She glanced between the boys.

"I hope you keep Pappy's spirit about women alive," she said. "He didn't buy into this skinny them versus plus-sized us. We're all women. We all hurt. We all want to feel beautiful. We all want to feel powerful in who we are. He believed in that. It's special what he's got here."

"We know that," said Lucas. "We both know that."

Scout was surprised to hear Lucas say something that benefitted both men. Gone was his competitive spirit and instead was…what the hell was that? *It's like he's protecting Josh.*

"Alright, look, gentlemen, I've enjoyed this, and I appreciate being invited, but I gotta run. I've got clothes to make and more coffee to drink," she said.

She got up and headed for the door as both men stood at her departure.

She turned back around. "Just one last thing," she said. She stared them both down. "Love or money?"

"What?" Lucas asked. "What do you mean?"

"Just answer the question," she said. "It's not hard."

There was a long pause as Josh looked out the window and Lucas looked at Josh.

"Money," Lucas said as he looked back at Honor.

"That's not a pretty answer," she said. "But it's the truth, I can tell."

She glanced at Josh. "And you?"

He finally turned his attention to her and just half-smiled.

"Interesting answer," she said. She took a sip of her coffee. "Alright, well, have a great day, you two. And good luck."

They nodded to her as she walked out.

"Josh?" Lucas asked.

"I'll see you in an hour at the next meeting," Josh said. He glanced at Scout with a terse smile, then walked out.

"Josh," Scout said as she stood. She felt a gentle hand on her arm and turned her attention to R.J.

"Let him go, Scout," he said.

She looked to Lucas, who nodded in agreement.

"Now," R.J. said. "Sit down and tell me about this offer."

"Offer?" Lucas asked. "What offer?"

"Well, come sit down and find out," R.J. said.

Scout sat back down as Lucas joined them. When both men turned their attention to her, she took a deep breath and spilled the tea about StudioX.

18

Wild and Crazy

Josh was having a hard time focusing on meeting number five—Robyn—even though his career, in part, depended on her.

He gave her a once-over. She was thirty-five years old and was supposed to be banishing the stereotype that plus-sized women have nicer personalities because they have to, or else people won't like them. Josh thought she was doing a great job.

Robyn was a consummate professional and beyond. She was dressed simply, wearing a white, button-down shirt from last year's line and fitted, black dress pants with basic boots.

Josh was all for women being strictly business, but in this case, Robyn went a touch beyond that, bordering on rude. She hadn't said a word to him or Lucas since they sat down because she was on her cell phone. At the same time, she was watching the stock market on a restaurant TV and ordering a salad from one of the waiters.

"Robyn?" Lucas interrupted.

When she held up her finger at Lucas, Josh rolled his eyes and immediately turned to look for Scout.

There she is.

He was melting from the inside out every time she flashed those burgundy lips at him. Then he glanced at R.J. *And dad knows it.*

Robyn said into the phone, "That's right. Move a million and when I get back, we can figure out the rest. Thanks."

She hung up the phone as the waiter handed her a salad.

"Thank you," she said matter of fact. She looked at Josh. "Josh, right? And Lucas?"

She shifted her stare from one to the other. They barely nodded when she said, "I

would have waited for you, but I don't have
all day for this. I've got exactly thirty
minutes. So, shoot."

"Uh, sure, yeah," said Lucas. "How are
you associated with Double Digits?"

"I'm not," she said as she prepared her
salad, carefully cutting and sliding and
pouring on dressing. Very utilitarian. "I
know Paps. I advised him on his finances.
He enlisted me to help with a few aspects of
his will. To get my thoughts. Next question."

Lucas and Josh glanced at each other as
Lucas shrugged.

"What did you think of Paps?" Josh
asked.

"Think of him?" she asked, as though to
think of a person as anything other than
another transaction was inconceivable.

"Yeah," Josh said. "Did you like him?
Hate him? Did you like the business?"

She stopped what she was doing and looked at Josh thoughtfully for a moment. It was the warmest she'd been since they sat down.

"He was a good man," she said. "I was happy to help him."

And then she went right back to her salad. *That's probably warmth for her.*

"He must have trusted you," Josh said. "Especially with his will."

She took a bite of her salad and nodded as she chewed.

"He did," she said after she swallowed her bite. "He was no bullshit. He wanted it straight. And that's what I did. He appreciated that."

Josh wasn't sure why, but somehow, he was now starting to like her. Once he saw what Paps probably saw—someone who was trustworthy and loyal—damn it, he liked her.

"He sure did," Josh said.

She finally looked up and gave Josh a smile as she relaxed a touch. She peered between them then landed on Josh.

"Taking over your grandfather's business must be stressful," she said. "Are you worried?"

She went right back to her salad and checked her watch.

"Carrying on his legacy is something we take very seriously," Josh said.

"Very seriously," Lucas added.

She glanced between them and nodded.

"It's a big job. A lot of people to think about. A lot of families who need their jobs," she said. "I deal with money and numbers, but trust me, I know, at the end of the day, there's a face behind every dollar sign. You should know that, too."

"We do," Lucas said.

"We do," Josh added. "We'll approach it in a very similar way that you approach your pediatric AIDS nonprofit. Working smart, making the right cuts and sacrifices. Surrounding ourselves with the right people."

Robyn stopped and smiled at Josh. "How'd you know about my nonprofit?"

"We did our research," Josh said, pointing between him and Lucas. Lucas looked confused but kept up appearances.

"Paps donated time and money to us," she said. "He was a smart man. Solid heart."

"Indeed," Josh said.

Robyn looked at her watch and said, "I've got a 1:30, Josh. It was a pleasure to meet you. And you, Lucas."

She stood up quickly, threw her salad away, straightened herself up, and shook both their hands.

"Nice to meet you as well," Josh said.

"Yes, it was," Lucas added.

"Good luck," she said as she turned and walked away.

Lucas peered at Josh. "I didn't do any research. I didn't know anything about that nonprofit."

"Well, now you do, little brother," Josh said. He slapped Lucas on the shoulder.

If Josh was going to bow out, and that possibility was starting to take shape in his mind, he wanted Lucas to be prepared.

Lucas must have sensed that because he said, "Josh, I—"

"I have something I need to do before our next meeting."

With that, Josh smiled at Scout and then turned and walked away.

Josh pulled up to the pond house, empty now, in the middle of the day. It was perfectly still and quiet.

He parked in his usual spot and just sat for a moment staring at the pond. He stepped out of the driver's side and put his keys in his pocket, then stepped to the back of the Cherokee opening it up and pulling out a canvas bag with plaint splatters. His mother's.

He grabbed a canvas and an easel, slung the bag over his shoulder, and headed for the pond.

As he set up the easel at the water's edge, he noticed how much smaller it felt now. And yet, it looked exactly the same as if he was eight years old again and his mother was right there next to him.

He took out a brush and a paper plate from the bag. No one had touched this bag since she died. She likely had put these materials in there herself. He couldn't help but feel closer to her now knowing her fingers had carefully picked out this very brush, placed it in the bag, used it many times, and put it back, thinking she'd paint one hundred more canvases with it.

He took a deep breath and let out a slow exhale as he focused on the reeds swaying in the wind.

"Why do the reeds remind you of me?" his mother had asked him later that night when she had put him to bed.

"Because, Mommy," he had said. "They're wild and crazy."

She had laughed at his young mind's reasoning and thanked him for the compliment. He realized now that what he'd meant was that she was pliable but strong just like the reeds. Growing in the sun, the water, and the wind, wild in nature, but beautiful.

His father, in contrast, was the pristine and structured landscape surrounding the house.

I'm like my mother.

That was the biggest bombshell of all. All this time, he grew up thinking he was like his father, and acted as such. But it wasn't true. Sitting here, painting the reeds, he realized he was like her. Her wild spirit was his. But when she died, that zest for life died with her.

Josh, instead, had done what his father needed from him after her death. And then, instead of growing out of it and into he who he was, he'd stayed there, in that place of grief, and let it sow inside him.

Scout.

When she slammed that coffee into him, he'd looked into her eyes and saw something that awoke the side of him he'd buried with his mother. Awoke it in a way he hadn't anticipated. Forced him to conjure it back to life.

He flipped the paper of the canvas and started a new painting.

Scout was warm and open but driven in a way he appreciated. She was intelligent and her business acumen was alluring.

And her eyes. Oh, those eyes. He could, and had, melted into them. When he was near her, all he wanted was to touch her, to run his hands over her body and sink into her lips with a kiss that would ensure she never wanted to leave his arms. He wanted to run away with her, take her on adventures. He wanted to be wild with her. He wanted to be himself with her.

I'm falling in a big, big way.

He looked at his painting and smiled.

I don't want to run Double Digits.

He felt tears prick the back of his eyes.

If he was honest with himself, and he was finally in a place where he was willing to be honest with himself, the reason he loved the company was because he loved Paps. He loved his grandma, who took care of them all after his mother died. And he wanted to honor that.

But what he really loved was his mother. What she had brought to their lives before they lost her. She brought love. So much love. And when she died, the love turned to pain, and it consumed them all. It seemed as though all her joy and light had gone with her. It would kill her to see them this way.

Well, not us. Me.

Lucas was exactly Lucas. Nothing more or less. He had, somehow, found a way to turn his grief into something like happiness. And his father had found Katherine. It was

Josh who had never found his way out of the grief.

He put the final touches on his painting and knew what he needed to do.

He looked at his painting of the sky and knew for the first time in his life he was headed in the right direction.

19

On Par

Scout kept an eye out for Josh as the late afternoon slowly found its way into early evening.

Jaime, twenty-seven, waited patiently by the food truck in the park. Her tall, athletic, but curvy, figure stood confidently in the crowd as her golden blonde waves floated lightly in the wind.

Where is Josh?

She glanced at R.J. and Lucas nervously as they smiled back at her. How was she going to tell Josh about the talk she had with them? Would he think she'd betrayed him? That *they* had betrayed him?

She felt a touch at her waist and turned to stare into Josh's eyes.

"Hi," he said quietly.

"Hi," she said.

He looked at his father and brother. "Get this over with?"

"Let's do it," Lucas said.

As Lucas walked away, Josh leaned down to her ear and whispered, "Can we talk later?"

She gazed into his eyes and saw nothing but warmth. It made her gut twist with regret. "Yes," she whispered.

"Good," he said. He smiled and slowly walked to Jaime. She twisted to R.J.

"R.J., I don't think—"

"It's going to be okay, Scout," R.J. said. "Trust me."

She wanted to trust him, but she felt very torn between her career and her burgeoning feelings for Josh. And more than that, she could feel that Josh was struggling, too. Although, his demeanor just now felt much calmer and more peaceful. Maybe R.J. was right. Maybe it would be okay.

She eyed Josh as he and Lucas took care of the final meeting.

Josh walked up and immediately was drawn to Jaime's friendly demeanor—and he noticed Lucas was, too. So much so, that his talkative little brother was rendered near speechless. In the absence of his brother's chattiness, Josh stepped up.

"Hi, Jaime?" Josh asked. He held out his hand.

"Hi!" she said, taking his hand and giving it a solid shake. "Josh, right?"

"I am," he said letting go of her hand. He peered at Lucas to give him an opening. Nothing. "Annnd this is Lucas."

Josh gave his brother a questioning look as Lucas finally spoke.

"Hi, yes, sorry, I'm Lucas," he spit out. He took her outstretched hand into a shake and let go with a smile.

"Nice to meet you," she said with a warm, open laugh.

Oh boy. I can't believe it. Lucas is bit by the bug.

Josh smiled with joy. *Finally.*

Jaime said, "It's so beautiful out. I thought we could take a walk and eat food truck food. What do you guys think?"

"Perfect," Lucas said brightly. "Uh, allow me."

Lucas pointed to the truck and he and Jaime walked together to get some hot dogs and fries. Josh glanced back to Scout and R.J. with a knowing smile, wiggling his eyebrows. His heart clenched with joy when he saw Scout smile at him.

His gut reacted equally when he saw his father smile. It was maybe the first genuine, knowing smile he'd ever gotten from his father since his mother passed.

Looks good on you, dad.

Josh turned back to the food truck and walked up to get his hot dog. He eyed Jaime for a second. She definitely shot down the sixth stereotype: Plus-size women are just not healthy nor athletic.

From his research, he knew that Jaime had been a competitive athlete at one time.

"So, Jaime," he said. "What was it like being a competitive swimmer?"

"Wet."

The three laughed as she smiled at Lucas, her hair blowing lightly around her bright face. *I have never seen that look on Lucas.* Josh smiled at his little brother.

"It was tough," Jaime continued as they each took their food. "It was my life. All I knew and did."

They walked together to a picnic table and sat down. As they started to eat, she continued.

"So, when my ex-husband, Danny, came along, I jumped at the chance to fall in love with something other than the swim lane."

"You were married?" Lucas asked.

"I was."

"What happened?" Josh asked. "I mean, if it's not too personal, I don't—"

"It's okay, I don't mind," Jaime said. "Press has covered my career and its collapse, so nothing you can't find by just Googling it."

"Gotcha," Josh said knowingly. He knew that life, too. He and his family had been covered ad nauseum by the press. Even now, the rumors and innuendos about the company and its future were everywhere.

For the most part, they ignored it, having gotten used to it. It was easy to forget sometimes that people knew more about you than you did.

"So, about a year after we got married, I got pregnant," she continued. "With my career on pause, I went a little nuts, eating for two, gained a ton of weight. Lost interest in anything that didn't have to do with my pregnancy and, eventually, our newborn son. Casey. This is him."

She pulled out her phone and showed Casey's picture to Lucas first. *She likes him, too.*

"He's beautiful," Lucas said. "He has your eyes."

She smiled at Lucas and there was a moment between them as she said, "Thank you."

Then, almost as an after-thought, she showed it to Josh.

"Cute," Josh said as she put her phone down. A look passed between the brothers and Lucas gave a shy smile before turning back to Jaime.

"Then what happened?" he asked.

"Well, you know, as a mom, I devoted myself to my son, and forgot to take care of my marriage," Jaime said. She gave a shrug of guilt.

"A marriage takes two people," Lucas said.

She snapped her attention back to him with a smile. "You don't have to say that. My game wasn't up to par—"

"You were taking care of your son," Lucas said. "Your game was on par. *His* game was the one that was lacking."

Josh eyed his little brother. *Way to go Lucas.* It was the most mature thing Josh had ever heard Lucas say and he knew exactly why he was saying it.

Their father. The good thing about R.J., the thing both sons appreciated about the man R.J. was outside of being their father, was that he loved and supported their mother. And now, Katherine. There was never any doubt about that. Paps had been a loyal and honest man. R.J. was, too. And now, it seemed, that sentiment was flowing through the brothers as well.

"Thanks, Lucas," Jaime said. She eyed him gently as another warm moment passed between them. "Well, uh, anyway...we got a divorce, I lost a ton of weight, started dating again, but..." she trailed off and shrugged, giving an embarrassed glance to Lucas.

"What?" Lucas asked.

"I mean," she said as she pushed her food away. "I don't know. I never had body issues because I was an athlete. It's weird to be dating again and have them now."

"What body issues?" Lucas asked. "You're stunning."

Jaime blinked with appreciation as a slow smile spread across her face.

"Thank you," she said quietly.

Suddenly, Josh felt very out of place.

"Uh, you know what," Josh said as he gathered his food. "I forgot, I have an appointment I need to get to."

"Josh, you don't—"

"Lucas, it's all good," Josh said. He could see on Lucas's face that Lucas felt bad he was going to win this vote. "Seriously. It is. You two enjoy the evening. Really."

Josh saw a smile of gratefulness cross his little brother's face. *This is the absolute right decision.* He turned to Jaime. "It was nice to meet you."

"You, too," she said.

They shook hands, then Josh gave Lucas
a slap on the back.

"Later little brother," Josh said as he
walked away. He looked at Scout and
walked toward her with a smile.

Whatever happened next, he knew Scout
was the key that had opened him up.

20

Meant to Be

Scout could barely catch her breath as Josh walked toward her. *My God, this man.*

"Hi," he said as he stood in front of her. He tossed his food in a trash can.

"Hi," she breathed out.

"On that note," R.J. said. "I'll leave you two to it."

"Wait," Josh said. R.J. turned to face him, and Josh enveloped him into a hug. "Thanks, Dad."

R.J. didn't say anything and when Josh pulled out of the hug she could see why. His father's eyes were glistening with emotion. All the man could manage was a slap to Josh's arm and a nod before he stuffed his hands in his pockets and walked away.

Josh turned back to her. "This has been a little crazy."

"You're telling me," she said.

"Scout, I—"

"Josh, wait," she said. She had to get this out, had to tell him the truth before it went any further. "I have a job offer with StudioX."

She saw the look of surprise on his face, followed by an almost immediate expression of being impressed.

"Wow," he said. "I mean, your work is incredible, so…that makes sense they'd want you."

She nodded. "It's the kind of job offer I've worked for since I graduated."

"I see," he said.

"The thing is," she started.

"Scout, you don't have to—"

"Josh, please let me get this out," she pleaded.

"Okay," he said. "I'm sorry. Uh, should we walk and talk?"

He glanced down the park at its tree-lined paths.

"Yeah," she said. "Let's."

As they started to walk, she was grateful for the cool evening, the trees, the people. It made the weight of their conversation feel lighter somehow. Gave them things to look at while they discussed the big issues at play.

What was happening between them was so new and yet, here they were, talking about things a couple in a relationship would discuss.

"It feels so strange to talk about this when we…" she trailed off.

"I know," he said. "All this and no first date."

He smiled at her, and she chuckled.

"I guess it's the kind of thing that determines whether we have that first date or not," she said.

"Probably does, yeah," he said. He gave her a warm once over. "Alright, talk to me."

"My offer at StudioX is a VP of Creative Services role with a leadership track to the C-Suite," she said.

"That's impressive, Scout," he said. "Is it something you want?"

She glanced sideways at him. She wanted nothing more than to kiss down his neck to his chest then to…*focus!*

"It is," she said. They locked eyes and she knew the depth of hers betrayed her. She could see in his eyes that he knew she really did want it. "StudioX is an incredible company."

"It is," he said quietly.

He glanced up as a young boy ran past him joyfully, followed by the boy's mother and father. The mother was pregnant. He smiled at them, and Scout could see a longing on his face. She wondered if it was the same longing she felt in her gut.

"After you left the coffee shop today, there was some confusion between your dad and I."

"Confusion?" he said. He stopped and looked at her.

"Oh, no, not bad," she said as she gave a little wave of her hands. "I tried to tell him about the offer, and he thought I meant the Double Digits offer and we got confused, and then we got clarity."

"Oh," he said. He started to walk again, and she followed. "So, you know then. About the offer on the company."

"I do," she said. There was a weighty silence between them for a moment. "How do you feel about it?"

He smiled. "I have mixed feelings about it."

"I understand that," she said.

He stopped and turned to her, so she stopped. And now she was face-to-face with the man who made her re-think everything.

"Scout," he said quietly. "I'm at a place now, thanks to my dad, where I can let go a little bit. Of the things that I thought I had to be and do. If I want to."

"Do you want to?"

He smiled.

"You know what. We're talking about *you* right now," he said. He turned and started walking again. She followed. *He wants to say something. What?*

"So, what else did my father say to you?" Josh asked.

"Oh," she said. "Uh, once he found out about my job offer, Lucas walked over, and we had a conversation."

"About?"

"My future. At Double Digits," she said.

Josh smiled. "Smart."

He looked at her with deep admiration. "I'd try and keep you here, too."

She melted at his stare and could barely get her words out.

"That's what he did."

"So, he matched the offer?"

"He did," she said. She smiled at Josh.

"I'd have done that, too," he said quietly. "For very different reasons, though."

He stopped and indicated to a bench on the path as twilight began its turn to night and a streetlamp next to them flickered on. She nodded with a smile and sat down as he took a seat next to her.

"Scout," he said. "We're both at really critical moments in our lives."

She nodded. And she wasn't sure why, but she wanted to cry. And also smile. And also kiss him and tell him to stop whatever he was about to say. *I want you, Josh.*

"I think you need to seriously consider both offers," he said. "That's what I'd tell my brother, or my friends, or anyone who asked me."

He looked at her with a sincere and business-like face. *I don't like that look.*

"Everyone should do what they love, and they should take great opportunities when they happen," he said. "And me…I'm actually kind of back at the beginning."

He smiled at her. "I have a chance to see what I want. For the first time in my life."

She felt her heart sink in her chest.

"Josh, I—"

"Scout," he interrupted. "I believe that when things are meant to be, they will."

His eyes blazed with longing as he looked into hers. "Do you believe that, too?"

She nodded, rendered unable to speak while he was looking at her like that.

"Then you need to make this choice for yourself," he said. "But I have a feeling you already knew that."

"Yeah," she said, finally able to say something. She felt the tears prick the back of her eyes as she took a sharp breath. She peered at him and saw his eyes had a sheen to them as well. "What do you think you want to do, Josh?"

"I'm not sure," he said with a sigh. "But I'm excited to figure it out."

He smiled at her. "What are you going to do?"

"I don't know yet," she said. "But I'm excited to figure it out."

Her phone dinged once, twice, three times.

"What the?" She looked down. "The votes."

She glanced at him.

"What?" he asked.

"Lucas won," she said.

Josh smiled broadly. "As he should have."

"Robyn voted for you," she said with surprise.

"Oh yeah?" he asked, impressed. "She's not so bad."

They sat together in peaceful silence.

She finally asked, "You're okay?"

"I'm okay," he said quietly.

He gave her a side-eye. "Remind me," he said. "What was the seventh stereotype again?"

"What?"

"You. You were the tiebreaker. And the seventh stereotype," he said. "Paps told us. I forgot. What was it?"

She chuckled. "That plus-sized women are just plain unattractive."

"Oh, well, hot damn," he said. "You put that stereotype to shame."

She laughed as she glanced at his face, humor and passion written all over it. She gave all the same emotions back to him in her stare.

"Do you really believe in meant to be, Josh?"

"I really do," he said.

A heat passed between them.

"I want to take the job at StudioX," she choked out.

He smiled as she composed herself.

"I think you should," he said.

"Josh—"

"Meant to be, Scout," he said. He put his arm around her and pulled her into his side. She breathed in his cologne and buried her nose into the crook of his neck.

I hope so.

21

What Do You Think?

Six months later

Scout walked confidently through the modern hallways of StudioX to her corner office that overlooked a thriving San Diego downtown core. The southern California city was adorned with every kind of holiday decoration possible. Christmas in warm weather was so strange. *I miss the snow.*

Her stiletto heels clicked against the white, glossy floor as her hips swayed back and forth in her classic red Valentino dress.

She carried a mocha latte in one hand and her cell phone in the other as she pondered her late morning meeting with a new nonprofit partner. *Who could it be and what could they have in mind for us?*

The meeting had been set by Scout's new assistant, Joy, who was a bright twenty-two-year-old with jet black hair and a brilliant smile. *Smart as a whip, too.*

Scout hadn't had a chance to miss Belle yet. Within a month of Scout moving to the sunny side of the country, Belle had come to visit and brought bags upon bags of cookies that she put in Scout's freezer. She also kept Scout in the loop on the Double Digits gossip. Lucas was really falling for Jaime, apparently.

A smile crossed her face at the notion, and passers-by returned her grin with varying levels of "hellos" and "hi there's." She was the boss now, and she loved it. Accepting the role at StudioX was the absolute right move. *For my career.*

She stopped at the large photograph that was hanging in the hallway just outside her office. Joy had put it there a month ago. The thoughtful assistant had searched for a piece of art to place there on the empty wall, at Scout's request.

It's so... captivating.

Scout wasn't sure why the piece resonated with her so much, or even who the artist was, but as soon as she saw it among the choices Joy had presented to her, she knew she had to have it.

"Mesmerizing, isn't it?" Joy asked.

Scout glanced over her shoulder at Joy with a nod before turning back to the landscape photo of Ireland on a foggy morning. "Stunning," she agreed. "Who's the artist again?"

"J. Quinn," Joy replied. She crossed her arms against her light blue cashmere sweater. "The art gallery didn't have much more info."

"Gotcha." Scout glanced at Joy with a smile. "So, who's my eleven with, anyway?"

"Oh, I'm not sure, actually," she said quizzically. "Debra told me to put the hold on the calendar and that's it."

"Weird," Scout said. "Does the CEO often just put meetings on calendars without information?"

"Not sure." Joy shrugged. "But let me find out what I can for you."

"Thanks," Scout said as Joy rushed back to her desk to get more information.

Scout turned back to the photo and stepped to the framed beauty. She lightly clicked the glass with her crimson-polished nail, then absent-mindedly glanced down to her phone and thumbed through the messages. *No Josh.*

After that night in the park, Scout had spent her final two weeks at Double Digits helping the brothers get everything in order as Lucas transitioned to CEO and Josh transitioned his duties to a new COO.

It had been a rough fourteen days, especially the day they cleaned out Pappy's office and moved Lucas in. The brothers and R.J. took turns telling stories about the patriarch and his irritating, but endearing, habits. Scout had been their captive audience, and they couldn't get enough of talking about the old days through laughter and a few tears that were hastily wiped away.

"I can't believe he's gone," R.J. had squeaked out. Scout had placed her hand on his arm, and he smiled warmly before swatting the tears from his eyes and pouring a whiskey neat for himself from Pappy's bar cart.

When he did, Scout had turned and picked up the black and white photo of

Pappy and Bessie. Josh had walked up behind her then and leaned his body into hers, burying his nose in the crook of her neck. She had felt a dampness on her upper back as a few tears escaped his eyes.

Other than that moment, they kept a very measured, and previously agreed upon, physical and emotional distance from each other before they went their separate ways at the end of June. September was when she heard from him again. Josh texted to ask how she was.

She had written ten different responses before landing on, "I'm okay. How are you?"

It was lame. But to tell him how much she missed him, how much she wanted him, would have been too much for them both. Instead, she turned the focus on him and his sojourn. "I've been all over the world, Scout," he had told her.

He had taken a few art classes, spent some time at the pond house, took a trip with R.J. and Lucas to Vegas, then another trip with just Lucas to his mother's hometown in Maine. "We ate so many lobsters," he had texted.

He, of course, only let her stay silent for so long before he finally forced her hand. She told him about the new job, how much she loved it and San Diego. She told him about a few restaurants and fun road trips she'd taken. "You'd love it here, Josh," she had texted.

"I know I would," he had texted back.

The last she heard from him was a month ago, a couple weeks before Thanksgiving, when he texted that he wanted to see her, that he was close to "figuring it out" for himself, and that he missed her. She took that opportunity to finally tell him she missed him, too.

And then nothing.

She exhaled a huge breath and focused on the Ireland photo again. The forefront was a quiet pond with lilies and swaying reeds. The background was rolling, green hills and a damp sky. It was black and white and stunning.

"What do you think?" a deep voice asked.

She would have known that voice anywhere. Felt its vibrato in her bones. Before she turned to stare into his eyes, she knew it was him.

"Josh," she said breathlessly. Her whole body felt like it was on fire as she slowly turned around and took in the man he was now.

His dark hair was mussed, and he had a bit of light scruff across his powerful jaw and chin. He was dressed casually in a blue suit, no tie, and dress shoes. His eyes had a much more confident glean to them, and they were lined with something else. *Peace.*

"Hi," he said lightly.

"Hi."

Every intimate part of her body was crying out for Josh to put his hands on her. She could feel the heat rising from the depths of her body, up her neck, and into her cheeks. Her lips parted as his lips did and she heard a small breath escape from his throat.

"Scout," he whispered. His eyes bore into hers as he took a small step toward her, that she returned. She briefly closed her eyes as the smell of his cologne wafted into her nose. When she opened them again, Josh was only a few inches from her.

He nodded to the photo. "What do you think?"

She had to shake her head at the change of subject before glancing behind her at it.

When she turned back to him, she could see a hint of pride in his eyes.

"Josh, did you take this?" she exclaimed.

He smiled broadly. "I did."

"No way," she exclaimed. "I love it."

He looked deeply in her eyes and gave her a warm smile. "Did you know it was me when you bought it?"

She shook her head. "My assistant gave me a few to choose from. I couldn't stop staring at this one."

He shrugged. "I wasn't sure," he said. "In all my traveling, I figured out photography is something I'm pretty damn good at."

"You are," she agreed. Then she gave him a tilt of her head. "But wait, the artist is J. Quinn?"

"Quinn is my mother's maiden name," he said. "Anastasia Quinn. I use Josh Quinn in my photography."

"Josh…" she whispered.

"It's a tribute to her, of course." He nodded. He turned his gaze back to Scout, pulled his hands from his pockets and placed them gently on her hips. He gave a gentle pull, and she moved closer to his body, gently holding on to his forearms. "I missed you, Scout."

She couldn't stop the tears that filled her eyes. "I missed you, too," she said. "So, what have you figured out?"

"Well," he said, pulling her even closer. "I figured out that I love business and I love running the Double Digits Foundation. I'm their new interim CEO."

"Oh, Josh, that's amazing."

"I think so." He grinned. *He looks so happy.* "I love working with the kids and the community. It's been an extraordinary opportunity."

"I love that for you."

"Thank you," he said. "I've also spent a lot of time with my dad and Lucas. Happy time, you know? Not grief. Or competition. Just, real quality time just being brothers, being father and son."

"You needed that."

"We all did," he agreed. "I also put a little grave marker by the pond for my mom. Spent some time there, and at Pappy's and Bessie's graves. I guess, you could say, I did some healing. Is that the right thing to say?"

She smiled and gave his arms a little squeeze. "If that's the way it felt, then yes, that's the right thing to say."

"It did," he said. He took a deep breath and let it out slowly as he pulled her in tight to his body. He was only an inch or so from her face now. "But you know the biggest thing I figured out?"

She slid her hands further up his arms as she pressed her body against his. "Tell me."

"I figured out that there's this amazing, successful girl in California I can't really live without."

She couldn't help but return the big, goofy smile that spread across his face as he gazed into her eyes.

"Oh yeah?"

"Yeah," he said softly. "And I figured it was about damn time I flew out to see her and take her on a first date."

She smiled as she waited for his lips to meet hers, until it hit her.

"Josh, wait, shoot, I have a —"

"A meeting?" he asked. She nodded. "That was me. I called Debra and asked her to put the hold on your calendar. You know. Just in case you said yes. I didn't want you booked up with someone else."

She grinned. "Well played."

"I can't take the credit. It was Lucas's idea," he said. He chuckled.

"Clever," she said. "And he'd know the tricks and tips. Although, I hear he's getting serious with Jaime."

"Well, if you call getting engaged serious."

Her face lit up. "What?"

He nodded. "They're getting married in the spring."

"Oh my God." She laughed. "That's so great. And fast."

"When you know, you know," he said. His eyes melted every cell in her body.

"So, about that first date," he said. His eyebrows danced. "Can I take you out to lunch and maybe a walk after?"

She smiled at him as her gut flared with bright bursts of joy.

"I mean, you do still believe in meant to be, don't you?" he asked.

His hands gently squeezed her waist as he leaned in close.

"Oh, you better believe I do," she said as she leaned into him.

"Yeah," he said. "Me, too."

As his lips took hers into a deep kiss, she slid her hands around his neck and held on.

And this time, she swore, she would never let go.

If you loved Scout and Josh's romance and want more, don't fret, it's coming! Follow Scout, Josh, Lucas, and Jaime in Books 2 and 3 of the *Double Digits Pocket Romance Series* by Author Steph West! Book 2, *California Love*, and Book 3, *The Pond House*, are coming soon. Check out the series by scanning below.

Scan me

<u>Review this book!</u>

Did you love *Double Digits*? Then let the author know! Leave a review on Amazon by scanning below.

Scan me

<u>Follow Author Steph West!</u>

Want more from Steph West? Follow her on Amazon to keep track of her new releases by scanning below!

Scan me

www.ingramcontent.com/pod-product-compliance
Lightning Source LLC
Chambersburg PA
CBHW021043310726
48969CB00006B/1791